A NOTE TO READERS

While the Edwards and Wakamutsu families are fictional, the events they faced from July 1944 to November 1945 are real. During the last years of World War II, people of Japanese heritage were released from relocation centers and internment camps and allowed to return to their homes on the West Coast. They often faced prejudice because people who had lost loved ones during the war with Japan took out their anger on their Japanese-American neighbors.

At the same time, Americans were beginning to discover the horrible things that had been done to Jewish people and other minorities by the Germans. American and other Allied soldiers freed prisoners in concentration camps. They learned that millions of people had been tortured, starved to death, and killed in gas chambers in these camps.

Most people call World War II a "just war" because it was a battle against true evil. While we may not be involved in military battles, we can choose to fight against evil every day when we see bad things being done to others in our neighborhoods and schools.

SISTERS IN TIME

Laura's
Victory
END OF THE SECOND WORLD WAR

VEDA BOYD JONES

BARBOUR
PUBLISHING

Laura's
Victory

To the memory of my father, Raymond E. Boyd—
World War II veteran. And to my husband,
Jimmie L. Jones—Vietnam veteran. Both are my heroes.

Cover design by Lookout Design Group, Inc.

Published by Barbour Publishing, Inc., P.O. Box 719, Uhrichsville, Ohio 44683
www.barbourbooks.com

Our mission is to publish and distribute inspirational products offering exceptional value and biblical encouragement to the masses.

 Member of the
Evangelical Christian
Publishers Association

Printed in the United States of America.

5 4 3 2 1

CONTENTS

CHAPTER 1

Eddie's Illness

Laura Edwards tiptoed across the wooden floor to her brothers' room. If Eddie wasn't awake, she didn't want to disturb him, but Mama had sent her to check on him. He'd had the sniffles and a headache for a couple of days now, probably catching a summer cold, Laura had decided. Nothing like when Eddie had developed rheumatic fever a few years ago, when he was eight and Laura was seven. With a high temperature, achy joints, a skin rash, and constant nosebleeds, he'd been miserable. For months, he'd had to stay in bed—and ended up missing so many days of school he'd had to repeat second grade, putting him in Laura's class from then on.

Yesterday, Mama wondered if Eddie was having another bout of the fever, which doctors had said could flare up at any time. But Laura didn't think so. He didn't have a rash or anything, and his nose looked fine to her. Knowing Eddie, he'd use just about any excuse to get out of making beds and cleaning the hotel rooms. When she'd peeked in at lunchtime, Eddie had been asleep. Unless his headache had gotten a whole lot worse, she expected him to have made a miraculous recovery and be up and playing, now that the last bed had been changed and the final room swept.

Fully dressed, her brother lay in the lower bunk bed with his eyes wide open, but he didn't sit up when she walked into the bedroom.

"Hey, Eddie, we finished the last room. You can get up now."

"I can't," he said in a terrified voice. "I've been trying to, but my legs don't work right." He lifted his head a little but didn't raise his shoulders off the bed.

"What do you mean?" Laura sat on the edge of the bunk. "You want me to pull you up?" She reached for his hands and was alarmed at how hot his skin felt. "You've got a fever." That surprised her. She'd gotten it in her mind that he'd milked his summer cold for all that it was worth. *Maybe the rheumatic fever has come back after all,* Laura thought.

"Look," he said. Eddie lifted his arm as if it pained him and pointed to his legs. Laura could see his legs tremble through his pant legs.

But that's not right. Rheumatic fever wouldn't make his legs shake. The next thing Laura thought of was the absolute worst thing in the world. *Polio.* "Oh, no!" she exclaimed. Every summer, Mama warned them to stay out of the heat of the day and away from the water. Wasn't that how kids got polio? But Laura hadn't heard of any cases this summer, and just a few days ago, she and Eddie had gone to the wharf to watch a troopship leave Puget Sound. They'd stood in the afternoon heat right by the water, that deadly combination.

"Get Mama," Eddie said. His voice still sounded terrified.

Laura bolted out of the room, nearly tripping over the cat. A sense of urgency propelled her through the living room and out the apartment door to the lobby. Mama was sitting at the desk in the office, talking on the telephone. Laura ran to the office window.

"Come quick!" she said breathlessly.

Mama held up one finger and continued talking.

"Eddie's real sick," Laura gasped.

Mama looked up, concern filling her features. "Excuse me," she said into the receiver. "Laura," she said carefully, "does his skin look funny? Is his nose bleeding?"

"No. . .but he can't move his legs."

Mama dropped the phone, then picked it up again. "Emergency!" she said toward the receiver and didn't even say good-bye before slamming it down. She dashed out through the office door and ran down the hall. Laura followed right behind her.

"Eddie!" Mama slowed down when she got inside the apartment and walked quickly to the boys' room. "Eddie!"

She leaned down on the bed and touched his face with the back of her hand. "You're burning up. Can you squeeze my hand?"

Tremors shook his arms. Laura watched the muscle spasms and saw her mother's face turn white.

"Mama?" Eddie said. "What's happening to me?" Panic colored his voice.

"Laura, ask Maude to pull her car around, and find Gary," Mama said.

Laura raced to the hallway again, pounded on Maude's door, and then ran to the back door. Fifteen-year-old Gary had been in the alley behind the hotel after lunch, and he was still there, talking to some other high school boys.

"Gary! Come quick! Something bad is wrong with Eddie." Laura didn't wait for her brother. She left the screen door standing open and ran back down the hall. Maude stood in the doorway of her apartment.

"Eddie's real sick. He can't move his legs," Laura said to Maude. "Mama needs your car."

Maude Bowers had been living in one of the apartments for some time now, and the Edwardses had grown to love her. Her car was actually her son's car. He'd left it with her when he went to war.

Maude grabbed her car keys off the key hook by her door.

"How long has he been sick?" she asked as they scurried down the hall.

"He hasn't felt well for a couple of days, but when he wanted to stay in bed this morning, I. . . .I thought he was just ducking his chores."

The back screen door slammed shut, and heavy footsteps thundered down the hall. Laura held the apartment door open for Maude and waited a moment for Gary.

Mama stepped into the living room. Her face was still unnaturally white, and she held on to the couch. "Laura, call the doctor and tell him we're on the way to the hospital," she said in a hushed voice. "The number's in the office. Maude, can you drive us? Gary, you'll have to carry Eddie. He can't walk." A sob choked her voice. "He was all right this morning, except for a headache. No signs of rheumatic fever. He didn't mention his legs hurting. It just seemed like a summer cold, nothing more. . . . How could this happen so fast?" Mama shook her head, gained control, and held up her hand as Maude moved toward her. "I'm all right. Let's take care of Eddie. Laura, can you manage the office? Can you handle that? The girls will be back sometime soon."

Laura sprang into action and raced to the lobby. The office door was still standing open. She went inside the small room and located the doctor's number on the important numbers sheet that Mama kept beside the telephone.

In a trembling voice, Laura told the nurse about Eddie. She was just hanging up the phone when Maude flew by the office, her car keys held out in front of her as if doing that would cut a few seconds off her task of bringing the car around. She hadn't been out the front door but a moment when Mama and Gary walked around the corner of the hallway.

Between them, they carried Eddie. He was wrapped in a blanket even though the July sun had raised the temperature to at least eighty degrees. Laura focused on his eyes, which were enormous. They were wide, not with pain so much as with bewilderment. What was happening to him? Laura knew he was worried. She and Eddie were so close in age—only a year apart—and spent so much time together that she often knew what he was going to say before he said it. And she almost always knew how he'd react to things.

Laura stepped out of the office. She stared at him, and he stared at her, and an invisible cord stretched between them.

"You'll be all right," she said in an unnaturally loud voice. "I know you will."

He didn't nod, which was their usual signal to each other. Maybe he couldn't nod. Maybe the fever had drained him of his strength.

The little group made their way toward the top of the stairs. Outside, a horn honked. Laura glanced down to the street and made sure it was Maude's car. She raced down the stairs, held the front door open, and then darted ahead of them to the car and opened the passenger door. Mama slid into the front seat and held Eddie on her lap. He looked odd half-sitting, half-lying on her.

He was eleven and almost as tall as Mama. Gary shut the door and hurried around to the driver's side. Maude scrunched up and pulled the back of her seat forward so Gary could slide into the back. The door slammed, and they were off.

Laura watched until they disappeared out of sight. Then she turned and climbed the stairs to the second-floor lobby. She took her place in the office. There really wasn't much to do, which was good. Her breath still came in gasps from all that running, and her heart was heavy with worry. "Dear God, don't let it be poli—" She couldn't say the dreaded word aloud for fear that it would make it real. "Please let him be all right."

She should call Dad, or was Mama doing that? They rarely called the Boeing airplane plant, and Laura didn't want to be the one to tell Dad anyway. What about her sisters?

Corrine was at the clinic, rolling bandages to send to the war. Margie was at work at the Boeing plant. She could call Ginny, who, at seventeen, had gone over to a friend's house after they'd finished the hotel work. Laura looked for the number, but she couldn't find it and discarded that idea.

Okay, she was here, and she could handle this. It wasn't the actual sitting behind the desk that bothered her. Fear for Eddie clutched at her mind and at her heart. She glanced at the clock on the desk and turned on the radio, which was usually kept on for the war news. Mama must have turned it off earlier when she'd answered the telephone. Bing Crosby was singing "I'll Be Seeing You."

The downstairs door opened, and footsteps ascended the stairs. They had a full house, and no one was checking out today, so if it was a stranger, all she had to do was tell the person that there was no room available.

"You in charge today, young lady?" the mailman asked.

"For a while," Laura said.

He handed her a bundle of letters, then turned and made his way down the stairs.

Ten-year-old Laura had never sorted mail before, but she knew she could do it. The boxes were numbers, and most of them had names on them. With the housing shortage in Seattle, the Edwardses had more permanent renters than those who came in for only a few days. Apartment boxes were on the top row, then the hotel rooms. That was one of the improvements that Dad had installed once they had bought and taken over the hotel. Dad liked organizing things. That's what made him so good as an engineer. He liked details.

Dad enjoyed his job at Boeing and earned a good salary, but after Eddie's bout with rheumatic fever, the family had struggled to pay off the doctor's bills. With Eddie's complete recovery, the Edwardses bought and moved into the Seattle hotel less than a month after the bombing of Pearl Harbor.

Although Laura didn't really like doing all her hotel chores, she did like living in the city. And most of the hotel residents were now like family. *Family. . . What is happening with Eddie?* Laura wondered.

The little clock on the desk ticked, but there was no news from the hospital. Laura half-expected her mother to call. Or maybe there was no time. Maybe. . . No, she wouldn't think the worst. *Think positive. Think positive.* She prayed for Eddie's recovery. She begged God to make him be all right.

Laura poked the thin letters into the boxes and had to force herself to keep working once she discovered a letter from her brother Bruce in the pile. She quickly finished putting up the mail and then pulled scissors from the desk drawer. With the sharp edge, she unsealed the letter. The paper was so thin, she didn't dare risk tearing it, for Bruce would have written over every inch.

Her oldest brother was a pretty good war correspondent. This time the letter was whole. There were no words that had been cut out. He hadn't written anything the censors would remove with their razor-sharp instruments. Laura had seen censors at work on the newsreel at the movies. Troop movements were too important to have leaked in case letters fell into enemy hands. The letters the family got from Bruce were written weeks, even months, earlier. Sometimes they would receive more than one letter a day. Sometimes they wouldn't get anything from him for several weeks.

She searched the top of the letter and found what she was looking for—June 16. He had written the letter after the D-Day invasion! The family had been waiting and waiting for news. After Laura had seen newsreel footage of the Normandy assault, she had understood the danger soldiers had faced. But if Bruce had been part of D-Day, he'd made it through alive and well!

She celebrated that news in her heart and listened to the clock on the desk *ticktock, ticktock.*

"Mail come?"

Mr. Arnold from apartment 15 stood at the office window, and Laura was glad she could hand him a letter. His grandson had been headed for England when he left, but now Mr. Arnold figured he was in Italy or France.

Mr. Arnold lovingly fingered the thin letter. "So Dale wrote his old grandpa." He gave a pleased smile and shuffled back to his room. The next time she saw him, he'd tell her everything Dale had written. He always did.

Laura read and reread Bruce's letter. He was doing fine but was looking forward to a home-cooked meal when the war was over. He was tired of the rations the army gave him. And he was tired of walking in mud.

Where is Bruce? Laura wondered. She wanted her brother home again and safe. She glanced at the clock. Not quite an hour had passed since Eddie had been taken away. What was the doctor doing to him now? She wanted Eddie home and safe, too. She wished she hadn't accused him of trying to get out of cleaning the rooms. Eddie had never liked the hotel chores.

Mr. Clauson wheeled down the hall in his wheelchair and collected his mail, causing a small stampede down the halls. Once the mail came in, word traveled fast through the building. Mama had once commented on how glad she was when she could hand mail over to the residents instead of telling them there was nothing for them.

"You'll probably get news tomorrow," Laura told disappointed residents. She imagined Mama had told them that before. And she knew how they felt. She wanted news of Eddie right now.

Why didn't Mama call? Would the doctors have put Eddie in an iron lung? No, that was the worst. Surely he could breathe on his own. She would think the best. For the hundredth time since Eddie had been carried to the car, she sent a prayer heavenward.

The clock on the desk went *ticktock, ticktock.*

A man with an old plaid suitcase climbed the stairs and asked for a room, and Laura suggested another hotel down the street. She listened to a special radio program on the V-1 flying bombs that Germany had launched on England. No roar of planes overhead had warned the people that bombs were coming. The first bomb had made a buzzing sound and then exploded, flattening two hundred homes at one time.

Would the Japanese launch the V-1 bomb on Seattle? Fear tightened its grip on Laura's heart. She took deep breaths and watched the minute hand slowly move on the face of the clock.

Another hour passed. Finally she heard Ginny's voice drift up the stairs. Corrine was with her, and it was clear from their footsteps that they were slowly making their way up to the lobby.

Laura wanted to shout at them to hurry, but what for? There was nothing they could do but wait for news. She watched the stairs until their heads appeared. They didn't resemble each other at all. Corrine was blond like Mama, and Ginny had curly dark hair like Dad and Laura. And Eddie.

Laura had remained calm while time had crawled by all afternoon. But now with her sisters there to give her support, she felt a great sob rise up from her heart to her throat.

"Eddie!" The name was barely recognizable as she said it through tears.

"Laura! Where's Mama?"

"What's wrong?"

Both girls spoke at once, and Laura's tears rolled down her cheeks. When she could talk, she told them Eddie's symptoms.

Corrine gasped. "Poli—"

"Don't say it!" Laura interrupted. "It can't be. We were only at the wharf the day the troops went out, and he didn't play in the water." That was what Mama constantly warned them about: "Stay out of the afternoon sun, and don't get in the water." Laura knew that warning by heart. But Eddie couldn't have the dreaded disease because even though the day had been warm, the sky had been overcast that afternoon. It had rained before they got back to the hotel.

The girls took turns standing at the window, sitting on the desk, and sitting in the lone chair behind the desk. They stared at the phone while the clock continued to *ticktock*.

When Laura didn't think she could stand it anymore, the downstairs door opened, and she heard familiar voices.

The girls rushed out of the office to the stairs. Below were Maude, Mama, and Gary. No Eddie.

They didn't say a word until they reached the lobby.

Her voice full of weariness edged with fear, Mama said, "It's polio."

CHAPTER 2

Laura's New Job

"No!" Laura cried and flung herself into Mama's arms.

"It's not as bad as it could be," Mama said. She patted Laura's back and rested her cheek on Laura's head. "The tremors are just in his legs now."

"Is he in an iron lung?" Laura looked up at her mother, hoping against hope that Eddie wasn't having a machine breathe for him.

"No, honey. His lungs are still okay, but he's in a special ward."

"Can we see him?" Ginny asked.

"Only through a glass divider. Girls, we have work to do. We must burn his bedding and scrub anything he's touched in the last two days. Laura, can you take care of the desk for a while longer? Did you get the mail sorted?"

Laura drew away from Mama's arms. "It's all put up." She went back into the office as Mama and the girls, followed by Gary and Maude, walked down the hall, dividing up the chores of disinfecting the apartment.

What about the rest of the hotel? Was everyone exposed to polio? Maybe everyone would move out. Then what? Would her family have to sell the hotel? And what about the Wakamutsus—the Japanese family who used to live in the hotel? They were in a relocation center in Wyoming now, upon orders from President

Roosevelt. What if the family made their way back to Seattle and found the entire hotel empty?

Laura really didn't know them that well, but she knew Mama and Dad valued their friendship. Her parents had first met Mr. and Mrs. Wakamutsu when the Edwardses bought the hotel in January 1942. Back then, Mr. Wakamutsu was working at the lumber mill. He and his family had been living at the hotel for several years.

Unlike many other people who feared the Japanese after the bombing of Pearl Harbor, Laura's parents didn't feel threatened by the Wakamutsus. In fact, Mama said Mrs. Wakamutsu was a big help to her when she was learning the ropes of running the hotel.

A few months later, all Japanese-Americans were required to evacuate Seattle and go to relocation centers and internment camps across the country. Mama and Dad were very sad to see the Wakamutsus leave. Although they had been gone for over two years now, some of their belongings were still here, packed away and waiting for them to return.

Well, the Wakamutsus and an empty hotel were the least of Laura's worries. And there was nothing she could do about either, so she dismissed those thoughts and concentrated on Eddie. She had asked God to not let him have polio. But God hadn't answered that prayer. Eddie had the dreaded disease. Would it do any good to pray that Eddie wouldn't be paralyzed? She didn't know, but she'd been taught to pray, so she did. She prayed as hard as she could that Eddie would be home soon, running and jumping, playing baseball, and trying to outdo her, just as he'd always done.

In an effort to take her mind off her troubles, she concentrated on the words and sang along with songs on the radio, and she handed out more mail as some of the residents returned from their jobs.

When nineteen-year-old Margie, dressed in coveralls, came in from her shift at the Boeing plant, Laura didn't tell her about Eddie. She'd let Mama do that. When Dad came home, she again maintained her silence about her brother. When he'd asked what she was doing in the office, she'd told him to go see Mama. She couldn't talk about it yet. She was too stunned by the terrifying news to do anything but block it out of her mind as best she could.

She gave out a couple more letters. Maude didn't have any mail from her son. And there sure wasn't any news for Corrine from her boyfriend. Neil Palmer had been missing in action for more than two years. Corrine hadn't given up hope that he'd return safely, but secretly Laura had.

"Laura." Dad stood in the doorway of the office. The fear in his eyes mirrored hers, and in two steps he had enveloped her in a huge hug. Once again Laura's fears overcame her, and she sobbed in her dad's arms. When her tears had subsided, he handed her his handkerchief. "How much mail is left?" he asked.

She glanced at the neat boxes. Only a few still held letters. "Four," she said.

"Let's deliver them, and then we'll close the office. We're going to the hospital to see Eddie."

"Me, too?"

"Especially you," he said.

Together they walked the halls and slipped the letters under the residents' doors. A few minutes later, the family loaded into Dad's car, and he drove them to the hospital.

"You can just see him through a window," Mama explained. "He's going to be all right. We have to believe that."

Laura wanted desperately to believe Mama. But could she?

Maude had said she must think positively about things. Think that Bruce would return safely from the war. Think that the United States would win the war. Think that life would return to normal. Now she could add to her list to think that her brother Eddie—her constant playmate and companion—would be okay.

At the hospital, the family huddled in the hallway to look through the large window, which was about six feet long and three feet high. Laura stood on tiptoes and peered through the glass. She spotted Eddie on the third bed. He lay on his back and stared at the ceiling.

"What are they putting on him?" she asked. Two nurses scurried from bed to bed and were now at Eddie's side.

"Hot, wet towels," Mama answered. "They're to help with the tremors, and we hope they will prevent paralysis."

Eddie must have felt their stares, for he turned his head slightly and looked right at them. His face clouded up, and Laura could see his tears even through her own tears.

"He needs us!" Laura cried.

"Yes, he does," Mama said. "Wave at him and smile. We must be strong for him." Another nurse walked into the polio ward, and Mama knocked on the window to get her attention. "Clifford, there's the one we need to talk to." She turned to the others. "Would you all wait outside? Dad and I will be out in a few minutes."

Gary held the exterior door for the girls, and they stood outside near the entry, waiting for their parents.

They talked about burning Eddie's sheets and clothes in the alley. One of the girls mentioned it was fortunate that he hadn't been anywhere in the hotel during the last two days other than their apartment and room 24—the room where Eddie had been painting walls and repairing screens with their brother Gary and Lee Bentley, the hired boy. Eddie hadn't contaminated the rest of the rooms. At the time, Laura had thought she was unfortunate, since she'd had to make up extra beds.

Mama and Dad joined them outside.

"What did you find out?" Corrine asked.

"What did the nurse say?" Margie asked.

"Let's get in the car," Dad said.

The group silently piled into the car and looked expectantly at Dad, who turned in the driver's seat to face them.

"His leg tremors are continuing. The head nurse thinks they will lessen soon, but we have to wait and see. The hospital is short-staffed right now, and your mom is going to stay at the hospital with Eddie. That means everyone must take on extra chores to fill in for her."

"When we get home," Mama said, "we'll make a list of chores and assign them. Since I won't be there to remind you, check off the chores as they are completed."

"Are you coming back here tonight?" Laura asked.

"Yes. Eddie's scared."

Laura nodded. She had seen that in his eyes. If she were in Eddie's place, she'd be scared, too, and she'd want Mama right beside her. But would that be dangerous for Mama?

Dad started the car. Laura remained silent for the ride home but listened to the others talk about dividing up the chores and making sure the hotel ran smoothly.

Back inside their apartment, Mama made a list of all the things she did. Laura had no idea there were so many things. Everyone was on room detail, which meant sweeping floors and changing sheets as usual. Corrine volunteered to take over the cooking, and Ginny said she'd be in charge of laundry. Laura was assigned to clean the hallways, lobby, and stairs every morning.

"I can put up the mail in the afternoon," Laura said.

Mama looked thoughtfully at her. "You did quite well today, even though you're young for the job. Corrine could open in the mornings, and if you take the afternoon office shift, then the girls could continue with their volunteer work." Mama nodded. "Okay, that's a good plan. But if you find you can't handle the office, Laura, you must tell Corrine or Ginny."

"I can do it," Laura said. And she felt confident that she could. She felt proud that she'd managed that afternoon, and she'd been under an enormous weight of worry then.

They divided up the other chores, with the older girls taking the biggest load, although Gary took his share. Mama packed a bag, and Dad took her back to the hospital. When he returned he looked weary, and the others gathered around him for any new word about Eddie.

"The doctor won't be back until tomorrow, but whenever she can, Mama will call the office to report on his condition. Now we must pray for Eddie's safety as well as Bruce's," Dad said.

"Oh, we have a letter from Bruce," Laura said. "He wrote it after D-Day. I'll be right back." She took the key from the nail beside the door and ran to get the letter. How could she have forgotten such an important letter? It wasn't that Eddie was more important than Bruce, but Eddie was here, and Bruce was—well, she didn't know where Bruce was. She wished she did.

Once Laura made it back to the apartment, Dad read the letter aloud. "I think it would be best if we didn't tell Bruce about

Eddie," he said. "Bruce has enough to worry about without us adding another burden. When Eddie is home again, then I'll let Bruce know what the family has been going through."

"But what should we say about Eddie? I always write Bruce what we're doing. Won't he think it strange if I don't mention him?" Laura asked.

"Tell him that Eddie is playing chess with your mom. She took the chessboard to occupy him. And another thing. . ." He looked at each one of them for a long moment. "I'll post a notice about Eddie's illness on the office door. If people ask, tell them that we've disinfected the area and that the hotel isn't under quarantine. We don't want a panic situation."

"We've only scrubbed our apartment," Corrine said.

"But we're about to work on the lobby and the stairs—the public areas. Thank the Lord that Eddie's movements have been limited to room 24 the last two days. Not counting Laura, Eddie is the youngest in the building, and polio usually strikes children, so our renters shouldn't worry unnecessarily. The danger of infection will be over shortly. But if you hear of anyone in the building being sick, we must alert them, in case they didn't see the notice."

Laura stared at her father. Without saying the words, he had told her that she was the most likely to get the disease. She felt her face. Was it hotter than normal? What were the signs? She wiggled her toes inside her shoes. They worked fine.

"Laura?"

She glanced at her dad and then at the others. Her sisters and brother had their heads bowed. She quickly bowed her own and added her fervent prayer that she, in addition to Eddie and Bruce, would be safe.

Dad wrote the notice and tacked it on the door, while the girls got mops and buckets and strong disinfecting soap and started on the stairs and lobby. Gary tackled the back staircase and mopped out room 24. Laura and Dad scrubbed the walls and floor of the hallways. They worked until nearly midnight, but when they were finished, every surface was clean.

First thing in the morning, Laura repeated her prayer for safety and checked out her legs. They worked. She hoped Eddie's muscles had stopped trembling and were moving normally by now. With a heavy heart and the weariness of worry, Laura, along with Corrine, Ginny, and Gary, moved quietly around the hotel, doing chores.

When the time came for her afternoon shift in the office, Laura grabbed an armload of books from the low table in the living room and carried them to the office. She wanted plenty to do while she was cooped up in the small area.

The time went by pretty fast. Her best friend, Yvonne Dreger, came by, and Laura explained that Eddie was in the hospital and she was taking over the office so Mama could nurse him.

Yvonne cried when she learned Eddie had polio.

"But we think it's a mild case, and he'll be okay," Laura hastily assured her. "He has to be."

She actually felt closer to Yvonne than to her sisters, since her sisters were older. Yvonne's brother Charlie had been killed at Pearl Harbor, on December 7, 1941, before Laura's family bought the hotel. Yvonne hated Japs with a vengeance, and so did Laura. How could she not hate someone who had killed Yvonne's brother? Mama told her that they should not hate, but they were at war. An enemy soldier could kill Bruce. Laura hated Germans, too, since it was more likely that Bruce was in Europe right now than in the Pacific. She wished she knew exactly where he was.

Yvonne promised to pray for Eddie and left for home. The mailman came, and Laura put the mail in the boxes and distributed it to residents who came to the office. There was no letter from Bruce, so she reread the one that had come the day before and wrote a reply. The Wakamutsus had written. She didn't open that letter, but Ginny did when she came to the office to see how things were going.

"Sachiko moved out of the relocation center," Ginny said, summing up the letter as she read. "She got a sponsor and a job in Chicago and was allowed to leave Wyoming. The family misses her, but they're glad she's no longer behind the barbed wire, like they are. The boys have organized a baseball team. That's just like them," she said with a smile. "They love baseball as much as Gary."

Laura was acquainted with the Wakamutsu boys—Minoru, who was Gary's age, and Kiyoshi, who was a year younger—but she didn't know them well. Oh, she'd been around them when their families had Sunday dinner together occasionally, but the older boys did things like play baseball or go the movies, so she and Eddie stuck together and played by themselves. Sometimes all the older children took Laura and Eddie and walked the streets around the hotel, window-shopping at various businesses located on the edge of the international section.

Suddenly the phone rang. It was Mama reporting that Eddie's fever was lower. That was a good sign. She didn't mention how his legs worked, and Laura didn't ask.

"How are you feeling, honey? Are you tired?"

So her mother was worried that Laura would get the disease.

"I'm okay. I've put up the mail and most of it is out." Laura told her about the letter from Bruce that had come the day before and the one from the Wakamutsus. "No one else is sick here," Laura told her. She had conscientiously asked everyone who came for mail how their family members were. So far, so good.

The days fell into a pattern. By week's end, Laura had settled into her new job. Yvonne came over in the afternoons and stayed an hour or so. She said she liked sitting in the small office, too, and might grow up to be a secretary. Mrs. Lind, who lived in apartment 8, came to the office precisely at four o'clock every day. That was when her favorite radio show ended. Every day she had a different complaint. Mama called about the same time each day to report about Eddie. The mailman maintained a fairly rigid schedule, too. No one in the building was ill, and Laura discovered each morning that all her toes and fingers worked. Maybe God was listening this time. Maybe He had been too busy listening to soldiers' prayers to hear her prayers about Eddie not having polio.

By the beginning of the second week, Laura was desperate for new activities to pass the long hours behind the desk. She missed Eddie. She missed playing with him, going places with him, even arguing with him. Listening to the radio while she was in the office did seem to help keep her mind off Eddie, but it didn't help her worries about Bruce.

"How's Eddie?" Yvonne asked when she came over. "Can he move his legs yet?"

"He's making progress," Laura reported. That's what Mama and Dad said. Just the night before the family had gone to the hospital to wave at him from behind the glass. This time he'd waved back, but one leg wasn't gaining strength like they had hoped. She didn't want to dwell on that and was glad when the radio program changed. "Oh, listen, it's news time."

As the correspondent talked, Laura wrote FRANCE in the margin of the newspaper. At supper she would relay the news she'd heard while in the office. Each night the family listened to war correspondent Edward R. Murrow report the latest battles, but first they got Laura's report.

"I wonder if Bruce is in France," Laura said.

"Why don't you ask him?" Yvonne suggested.

"He can't tell us. You know the censors would cut that out in a flash."

"Maybe he could give you hints."

Laura got Bruce's latest letter out of the drawer. "He mentions mud, but that could be anywhere. Before D-Day, the censors missed his letter because he mentioned a town in England, and it wasn't cut out. We looked it up on the map, so we knew where he was." She opened the atlas that she'd carried down to the office and showed her friend the exact spot. Bruce had written he'd gone to a movie when he'd had a rare night off.

Yvonne tapped her finger on the map. "Do the censors read your letters to Bruce?"

"I don't know. I could ask him where he is, but what good would that do? He can't tell us."

"He can't tell you town names or country names, but what if you made up a code?"

"A code! Yvonne, you're a genius! I can't believe I didn't think of that myself."

Laura pulled a sheet of paper out of the drawer. "I think our code needs a real piece of paper." Because of the paper shortage, they usually wrote on scrap paper, but this would be a code they could refer to every time they wrote to Bruce.

She was hungry, so she thought of food words. "For *France* we'll use *pie*." That was a treat they had not had since Eddie had gone into the hospital. Corrine said she was no good at making pies and had instead been saving the sugar so Mama could make a couple of them when Eddie came home.

"What about *steak* instead of *England*?" Yvonne suggested.

For the first time since Eddie had gotten sick, Laura felt excited and challenged. She eagerly set to work thinking of words for every country in Europe.

CHAPTER 3

Eddie's Homecoming

"How's Jerry doing?" Laura asked from the office window where she was working the afternoon shift.

Maude looked up from the letter she'd just opened. "It's hard to tell." She held up her son's letter. All the holes reminded Laura of the snowflakes she'd cut out for the school bulletin board last winter.

"Jerry wasn't thinking about the censors when he wrote this one. I can't make out a whole sentence. Listen to this. 'We rode down to the *blank* where Cecil Woodall had left the truck. The tires were a foot deep in *blank*. We thought we'd need it for *blank*, but the lieutenant said we'd have to *blank*.' There are more blanks in this letter than words."

"You need the code," Laura said and opened the desk drawer. She pulled out the code sheet that she and Yvonne had devised and handed it to Maude.

"You think this will work?" Maude asked after Laura had explained the system.

"I don't know. It's been three weeks since I sent it to Bruce, and we haven't had a letter where he used it. He probably doesn't have my letter yet."

"I need to add code words. Jerry shipped out of Seattle. If he went to the European front, he would have sailed from back East, not from here. What can we use for *Philippines* or *Hawaii* or other island words?"

Laura opened the atlas to the Pacific Ocean, and she and Maude made a new code. They used names of flowers for the various Pacific islands and chuckled as they assigned the new words.

It felt good to laugh. There hadn't been much to laugh about lately. Eddie was through the worst of his illness, and although Mama came home at night, she stayed at the hospital with him during the day, helping him with exercises.

The hotel was running smoothly, but the family had to work more hours to keep everything going all right. People moved from one job to another, and Dad had complained that there had been quite a turnover of workers at Boeing since war production had begun. That also meant people moved in and people moved out of the hotel, and there were more rooms to clean thoroughly.

Maude had helped a few mornings with the office so that Corrine could work in the rooms alongside the others. When Eddie came home, Mama would go back to mornings in the office when most of the checkouts occurred, and Eddie would help again in the rooms. At least, Laura hoped he would. The latest report from the hospital had not been that good, although Eddie was gaining strength day by day.

The phone rang. Laura handed the flower code sheet to Maude and reached for the receiver.

Mama's voice held guarded excitement. "The doctor says Eddie can probably come home on Friday. He'll still have to do his exercises, but he'll be home."

This was Tuesday. Three more days. Laura's heart repeated

the refrain. *Three more days. Three more days.* They could put up a big sign for Eddie, and maybe Corrine could bake a cake. Yvonne could come over, along with Eddie's friend, Kenny Howell.

"I'll tell the others," Laura said. "How's his leg?" One had been responding to exercises, but the other one still wasn't doing well.

"He won't be walking when he comes home, but maybe soon," Mama said. "We must hope and pray for the best."

"Any mail for me?" Mrs. Lind was at the office window, having nudged Maude aside with her large bulk, and she was demanding immediate action even though Laura was on the phone. Laura shook her head. "Well, do you have the newspaper?"

"I can hear Mrs. Lind," Mama said. "Better take care of her. I'll see you this evening, Laura."

"Bye, Mama." Laura hung up and handed the afternoon newspaper to Mrs. Lind, who never bought one of her own, but instead came down to borrow the hotel's copy of the *Seattle Times* every afternoon. The first time she'd acted like she was going to take it back to her apartment, but Laura had told her she had to read it in the lobby in case someone else wanted to see it. She didn't know if that was Mama's policy, but Mrs. Lind just grumbled and settled herself on the low couch, so Laura figured that Mama had told her that before.

Maude moved to the window again. She was the exact opposite of Mrs. Lind. Maude looked on the positive side of everything, which she always told Laura was the sunny side and the only way to be happy. Mrs. Lind could find wrong in everything and everybody. Those two women were night and day, breakfast and supper, sweet and sour. Laura grinned at Maude and shook her head.

"Eddie will be home on Friday. Three days."

"We must plan a homecoming party," Maude said. "How's his leg?"

In a sad, quiet voice, Laura recounted the little she knew.

"He shouldn't come home too soon," Mrs. Lind said from the couch. "He could still spread the disease."

"No, he can't, or the doctor wouldn't send him home," Laura said.

"Are you being impertinent, Laura Edwards?" Mrs. Lind asked.

"No, ma'am. I'm just saying what I think. Eddie hasn't had a fever for some time. Mama wouldn't bring him home if he could spread polio to the rest of us."

"I guess he won't be tearing around the place like he usually is."

Laura couldn't believe Mrs. Lind would actually say that.

"No. He can't walk yet," Laura said coldly.

Mrs. Lind had the grace to look flustered. "Oh, I didn't know."

"She couldn't have heard what you told me," Maude said in a low voice. "She didn't know."

"He'll walk soon," Laura said. "I know he will."

The next day when Yvonne came for her afternoon visit, she and Laura planned Eddie's homecoming party.

"We need a big banner," Yvonne said. She waved her hand in the air as if reading from a large invisible sign. "WELCOME HOME, EDDIE!"

"We don't have that much paper," Laura said.

"What else could we use to make it?" Yvonne asked.

Laura thought a moment. Gary and Ginny's high school had

a banner made of cloth that the band carried in parades. Maybe she and Yvonne could use a sheet for the background, but Laura didn't know of any scrap material they could use for the letters. She glanced around the office. The last few days' newspapers were stacked in a corner, waiting to be taken to the collection site.

"Oh, we can cut letters out from these newspapers and pin them onto a sheet," Laura said. "Then we can unpin them and use them for the paper drive."

Yvonne drew large letters on the newsprint, and Laura cut them out with the office scissors.

She paused to read a front-page story about the Americans capturing the island of Guam. She and Maude hadn't made a code word for *Guam*. They'd need to. The article summed up the war in the Pacific and mentioned in passing the horrible Bataan Death March when the Americans in the Philippines had surrendered to the Japanese more than two years ago.

"I think Neil Palmer is dead," Laura said. "Corrine prays about him all the time, and she keeps saying he's coming back, but I don't think so." If he had been captured, he'd have been forced to walk miles and miles, day after day with no food or water, and then put in a horrible prison camp. Laura didn't think he could last through that. "I hope he died in the fighting instead of having to go through all that torture and then die."

"He wasn't listed in the paper," Yvonne said and pointed to the daily column that listed names of the local men who'd been killed in the line of duty. She drew a big *E* on that page.

"Mama said the Japanese didn't sign some agreement, so they won't give out the names. That's why he's listed as missing. The navy doesn't know where he is."

"The dirty Japs," Yvonne said through gritted teeth. Her eyes shone with tears. "I hope every one of them gets killed." She sniffed. "Mama is okay most of the time, but yesterday she was fixing supper and she just sat down on the kitchen floor and cried. She'd been cutting up a chicken, and I asked for the wishbone, and she said when Charlie was my age, he always asked for the wishbone."

Laura didn't know what to do for her friend, whose tears were now running down her cheeks. She patted her on the back. Laura hadn't known Yvonne's brother. Her friend hadn't had any sisters, and now she didn't have a brother. Laura couldn't imagine what it would be like to have only her parents as a family.

"Do you have a handkerchief?" Yvonne asked.

Laura shook her head.

"I only have this one, but I can't use it." Yvonne pulled a lace-edged handkerchief from her pocket. Embroidered on one corner was a palm tree and the word *Hawaii*. No, she couldn't use the special one that Charlie had sent her.

"Use this," Laura said and handed her a scrap of newspaper left over from when she'd cut out the letter *E*.

Yvonne wiped her cheeks and blew her nose on the newsprint, which left black ink across her face.

"Oh," Laura said, "you should see yourself." She grabbed the small mirror that hung on the wall and held it in front of Yvonne. "Your face is streaked with black."

Yvonne's mouth dropped open, and she squealed. "I look like someone painted me!"

Laura thought Yvonne was going to start crying again, but instead she laughed. She hooted, and Laura felt laughter bubble up inside her. Soon the girls were laughing so hard, tears spilled from their eyes.

"Use this," Yvonne said and handed a newspaper to Laura. Laura wiped her cheeks and looked in the mirror. Her face matched Yvonne's.

"What's so funny?" Mrs. Lind stood at the office window. "What have you two gotten into?"

"Nothing." Through gales of laughter Laura asked, "Would you watch the office while we go wash up?" Not waiting for an answer, she opened the office door and dashed for their apartment with Yvonne right behind her.

When the girls returned to the office, they were clean, and Laura carried a sheet and a pin cushion stuffed with straight pins. Mrs. Lind was talking through the office window to a short man wearing a brown suit. On the floor beside him sat two suitcases.

"May I help you?" Laura asked and went inside the office. There was hardly room for her and the large woman beside her.

"He wants a room. Isn't 32 vacant now?" Mrs. Lind asked.

"Yes. How long will you be here?" Laura asked. She filled out a form just like Corrine had shown her, had him sign it, and gave him the room key. The man picked up his suitcases and headed down the long hallway. "Thank you for watching the office, Mrs. Lind."

"You're welcome," she said, but she made no move to leave the small room. "What are you making?" She waved to the newspaper letters on the desk and the pile on the floor where Yvonne had been drawing the letters.

Laura explained about the banner.

"You'd have more room if you worked out there on the floor,"

Mrs. Lind said, pointing to the lobby. "Stretch that sheet out across the couch to pin the letters on." Without hesitating, she handed the scissors and pencil through the window to Yvonne. "Here." She thrust the letters and the unused newspapers at Laura.

Mrs. Lind was one pushy woman, but this time she had a point. There was more room to work in the lobby. While Yvonne pinned letters on the sheet, Laura quickly cut out the remaining letters. By the time Yvonne had to leave for home, the banner was finished.

"Looks terrific," Yvonne said. "Where can we hang it?"

"In his bedroom, I guess," Laura said. "No, maybe in the living room. Mama says he has to do exercises, so he shouldn't be in bed too much." They folded the sheet, careful not to dislodge any pins.

"Tomorrow we'll plan the food," Yvonne said. "We need a cake. I'll see how much sugar we have at home. And I'll tell Kenny."

As soon as Yvonne walked down the stairs and waved from the bottom step, Laura went back into the office.

"Thank you for watching the office, Mrs. Lind. I'll take over now."

"Sure you don't have anything else you have to do?" Mrs. Lind remained seated in the desk chair.

"No, this is my job for the afternoon."

The phone rang, and Mrs. Lind grabbed the receiver. "Bayview Hotel... Yes... One moment... It's your mother," she said, placing the receiver on the desk.

Laura looked pointedly at the woman, and with reluctant movements, Mrs. Lind stood and walked out of the office.

"Thank you again," Laura called.

"Why was Mrs. Lind in the office?" Mama asked.

Laura explained. "I was only gone a few minutes, but it was hard to get her out of here."

"She's a lonely woman," Mama said and then went on to tell Laura that Eddie was doing very well.

"Good," Laura said. "We're planning a surprise for him."

"Oh, he's planning a surprise for you, too."

No matter how much Laura pleaded or cajoled, Mama wouldn't reveal the secret. Nor would she tell the family anything that evening when she came home.

The next afternoon, Yvonne and Laura worked on making more decorations. Since they didn't have balloons, they cut streamers out of more newspapers to tie in bows everywhere they could. Yvonne also announced that her mother had said they had enough sugar to make a cake.

Maude said she'd also make a cake to celebrate Eddie's return so everyone could have a big piece. Everything was set for the next afternoon. As soon as Mama called the office to let them know that Eddie had been dismissed, Maude would drive to the hospital and get them.

But the call came in the morning. Corrine was running the office when Mama phoned. The doctor had come early and dismissed Eddie. As soon as Maude could get there, he could come home. She left immediately for the hospital.

Daily work at the hotel came to a standstill. Laura called Yvonne, and she called Kenny. They both hurried over to the hotel, Yvonne carrying a cake fresh from the oven. Gary, Ginny, and Laura hustled about, hanging the banner, tying streamers on every chair, curtain rod, and candlestick in the living room.

They finished their work and rushed to the lobby to await the honk of Maude's car horn. The plan was for Gary to carry Eddie up the stairs, and then they'd all yell, "Welcome home, Eddie!"

"They should have been here by now," Ginny said after the welcoming group had paced the lobby for fifteen minutes and made countless trips up and down the stairs to the street below.

"Maybe they had a flat tire," Kenny said.

"Are you waiting for me?" Eddie said from the hallway. Mama stood beside him, and Maude stood behind both of them.

As one, the group turned toward his voice.

"Eddie, you can walk!" Laura exclaimed.

CHAPTER 4

Madam President?

Laura stared at Eddie then rushed toward him.

"Careful." Mama stepped in front of him before Laura could reach him. "He can't walk very well yet, but he wanted to surprise you."

Maude carried crutches and placed one under each of Eddie's shoulders. He looked less tense now that he had some support. Lines in his forehead smoothed out.

The others crowded around him.

"Are you in pain?" Yvonne asked.

"Can you go to school?" Kenny asked.

"Did you walk all the way up here from the back steps?" Gary asked.

"One at a time," Mama said. "We don't want to overwhelm him."

"I'm okay, Mama," Eddie said with some of his old forcefulness. He turned and took a few awkward steps down the hall toward the apartment.

"Mama and Maude carried me up the stairs to here. I'm not real good at walking yet, but I'm getting better." He touched the wooden crutch to his right pant leg, and Laura heard a clunking sound. "This brace under here helps keep my leg straight."

Laura's gaze shot to Yvonne's. They'd discussed the posters of polio kids with both legs in braces. Did a brace mean that Eddie would never regain use of that leg? Mama had said he was getting stronger. Didn't that mean that he would return to normal and be able to run and jump?

The group followed Eddie in a slow procession. Each of his steps seemed to take incredible concentration, and Laura found herself moving in the same way as Eddie with the same limp. She wasn't trying to mimic him, and she certainly wasn't making fun of him. She was trying to help—trying to take some of the burden from him, but she knew there was no way she could.

Mama held the apartment door open, and as soon as they were all inside the apartment, Laura gave the signal. Immediately everyone yelled, "Welcome home, Eddie!"

"We have cakes to celebrate," Laura said.

"I could eat a couple of pieces," Eddie said. "Maybe three."

Mama laughed. "Eddie's been without sugar for a long time." She helped him sit on the couch with his legs stretched out.

Corrine cut Eddie a big piece of cake, then took a piece with her and rushed back to the office. Ginny served the others, and they chatted with Eddie.

Laura wanted to cut all the chitchat and ask if Eddie would ever be able to walk without the brace. She knew he'd been having trouble with that one leg, but she'd thought that it would get stronger. Mama had mentioned time and again that Eddie was exercising it. Now it appeared that he had no control over it at all. Laura could see the ugly brace where his pant leg didn't cover it. She tried to look away, but her gaze kept coming back to his leg stretched out on the couch. Above his sock, the leg looked thin and bony. Tears stung her eyes, and she quickly got up and walked into her bedroom.

"Laura," Mama said from the doorway of the girls' room, "are you all right?"

"I thought he wasn't going to be crippled," Laura said. Her voice caught on a sob. "I thought he was going to be all right. But he isn't, is he?"

Mama crossed the room and hugged Laura. "He is all right. He's not going to die from polio. That he has to wear a leg brace is a reminder of how much worse it could have been. We should thank God that Eddie's not in a wheelchair like Mr. Clauson," she said. "Before long Eddie will be able to walk without crutches, and knowing him, he'll be running not long after that."

"With a limp."

"Yes, with a pronounced limp. But he'll be walking."

"I prayed that he'd be all right." Laura pushed away from Mama and plopped down on the bed.

"He is all right," Mama said once more.

"But I prayed that he would be back to normal. God didn't listen to me," Laura said defiantly and stood up. She couldn't sit still. She couldn't stand still. She wanted to strike out, to do something to release the anger she felt at Eddie being cheated by life—first by the debilitating rheumatic fever, and now this. At the beginning of the summer, he'd had a whole body. Now he had one shriveled leg.

"Laura," Mama said, "God listened, and He answered your prayer—but not with the answer you wanted. Good will come from Eddie being crippled."

"How can it?"

"I don't know, but when bad things happen to us, God sometimes uses the situation so that we can learn and grow as people. We must have faith." Mama handed a handkerchief to Laura.

"Now dry your eyes and go be with Eddie and your friends. Eddie needs you to be strong. Accepting that he will be crippled hasn't been easy for him, either. He's still fighting it. He hasn't given up on a miracle restoring his leg."

Laura sniffed and wiped her tears. "Me, either."

With her head held high, she walked back into the living room and talked with the others about school starting in a couple of weeks and about the ever-present war. She sat down on the floor beside the couch where Eddie lay. She needed to be near her brother after a month of being away from him.

"We've gathered tons of paper," Kenny said and looked purposefully at the banner made of newspaper letters.

"We can use those," Eddie said, "but not for a little while. I like seeing my name like that."

Yvonne laughed. "The Girl Scouts are collecting paper, too."

Laura had been so busy with hotel work and running the office in the afternoon that she hadn't had time to go out collecting. Instead, she'd made a place in the lobby for people to put their used paper.

"Oh," she said, "we didn't finish the rooms."

"How many are left?" Mama asked in the normal business tone she used for hotel matters. For an instant it seemed that things were back to normal. If only Eddie wasn't stretched out on the couch and could hop up and race Laura down the hall to finish their chores.

Reluctantly, Laura stood up. "Just a few. We'll be back within the hour," she said.

Mama left Maude, Kenny, and Yvonne to occupy Eddie, and she went with Laura and the others to finish cleaning the empty rooms and making the beds.

"Will Eddie be able to go to school?" Laura asked when they had finished the last room and were headed back to the apartment.

"If you help him, I think he'll be okay," Mama said. "He's got to practice walking. We can't risk him falling down. That could further damage his leg. But we can't let him baby it, either. Laura, you've got to work with him. Make him use that leg. The rheumatic fever already put him back one year. We don't want him to get even further behind in his schooling."

That afternoon, Laura convinced Eddie that he could walk to the office and keep her company while she worked her shift. Mama didn't offer to take over, so Laura figured that job was still one she'd do until school started. She carried an extra chair to use in the office while Eddie sat in the big chair behind the desk.

"I sort the mail like this," Laura said after the mailman had left a bundle of letters. She stood up and pointed to the boxes. "I match the names and the apartment numbers."

"Don't talk to me like I can't understand simple things," Eddie said. "Remember, I'm a whole year older than you, even if we are in the same grade. And I may be crippled for a while, Laura, but I'm not dumb."

"I never thought you were," Laura said.

"Hand me my crutches," he ordered.

She gave them to him, and he used them to stand up. "What are you doing?"

"I can put up the mail faster than you can," Eddie said.

"You can not," Laura retorted.

"Watch me," Eddie said, and with one hand on a crutch for balance, he pushed letters into boxes with the other hand.

Laura's mouth fell open, and she started to snap at him; then she grinned instead. Eddie was back! Good old Eddie, who tried to make everything between them a competition.

She watched him stuff the mailboxes. Although she did the job with a lighter touch, he may have been faster at it than she just because he wanted to beat her time.

"Now you have to give it out to people, and you have to do it nicely," she said. "They all want mail, and not everyone gets something. I'd better do that part. You don't want to tire yourself by sitting up too long."

"I'm all right. I sat up lots of time in the hospital."

"What was it like?" Laura asked.

"It was bad," Eddie said as he sat down hard in the big desk chair. "But there were so many who were worse than me. Most of the kids were alone and didn't have their moms with them. I heard Mama say she couldn't have been there if it hadn't been for the hospital being shorthanded and Mrs. De Wilde recommending her."

"Mrs. De Wilde, our principal?"

"Yeah. Her brother runs the hospital, so Mama got special permission to stay with me, as long as she'd help with other patients, too."

That was news to Laura. She'd assumed all mothers could stay with their children. From down the hall she heard the distinct heavy footfalls that signaled Mrs. Lind's afternoon trip to the office.

"Well, if it isn't Eddie back. You need me to work there so you can help him back to your apartment?" she asked.

"No, we're all right," Laura said. "No mail today, but here's the newspaper." She thought the woman would leave, but Mrs. Lind leaned on the counter in front of the office window.

"How are you feeling, Eddie? You all right? Can you walk?"

"I can walk pretty good," Eddie said, although Laura knew that wasn't true. "Just need some practice."

"Well, take care of yourself," Mrs. Lind said. She took the *Times* and settled herself on the couch.

"What happened to her?" Eddie whispered. He and Mrs. Lind had never gotten on very well.

Laura shrugged. "You going to practice walking? Mama says you've got to get real good if you want to go to school on the first day."

Eddie winced. "I'll walk to the apartment and get a drink."

"We ought to set up a schedule of walking," Laura said. "Could you walk the entire hallway today? Tomorrow you could do it twice. Then the next day three times." She could tell he was already tired from the excitement of coming home and sitting up for several hours, but Laura thought he would do better if he had a goal.

Walking the halls became the plan. During the first week, Laura walked beside Eddie as he plodded along. Sometimes Kenny came over, and he walked beside Eddie. Some days it was Yvonne who walked alongside him. Day by day, Eddie became stronger. Mama showed him how to take the stairs. There was a method of using crutches going down and a different way to use them going up. Eddie got good at it, but the knowledge that it was now so much more difficult than before made Laura sad.

A week before school started, Laura and Eddie changed the exercise from the hallways to the regular walk toward school. Each day they made it farther before they'd turn around and go back to the hotel. Laura had to hand it to Eddie. He worked hard at walking, harder than she thought she'd ever be capable of working.

Sweat broke out on his forehead sometimes, but he wouldn't give up. He kept walking.

Each afternoon, she and Eddie divided the mail and put it up. They talked of his disability, but Eddie was vehement that his leg was not permanently damaged. He said if he tried harder, he could make it well. At first Laura had agreed, but she had watched him gain strength in his arms from using the crutches, not strength in his bad leg. Now she didn't believe his leg would heal any more than she believed Corrine's boyfriend would come back home.

By the first day of school, Eddie was ready. He had convinced Mama and Dad that he could make it, even though Maude insisted on driving him the few blocks to school.

Laura and Eddie weren't in the same fifth-grade classroom. Yvonne was in Miss Burch's class with Eddie, and Kenny was in Mrs. Jamison's class with Laura.

"I'll take care of him," Yvonne whispered to Laura as they stood in the hall reading the list of students in each room. "I'll treat him like he was my very own brother."

Laura started to object, but decided that maybe Yvonne needed a brother. Not that she was giving Eddie away, but she was willing to share him with her friend.

Right after Mrs. Jamison introduced herself, she explained the air-raid procedure. For the last two years, Laura's father had assured her over and over that the Japanese couldn't fly a plane close enough to shore to bomb them. But she remembered that radio program about the Germans launching buzz bombs from long distances away. If one of those came, then the students wouldn't even have time to get underneath their desks.

How was Eddie going to get under his desk? He couldn't squat down like the rest of them. Surely his teacher was fixing some special place for him to be safe. At recess, Laura asked him, and he said they hadn't had air-raid instructions yet, but he'd make sure his teacher found a place for him.

At one end of the playground, a group of boys played kickball. Laura, Yvonne, and Kenny grouped around Eddie and talked about everything they could think of except the kickball game. Eddie kept glancing at the boys with the ball, and Laura saw a grim determination light his eyes. He shifted on his crutches when the ball got away from the boys and came straight at him.

"I can kick with my good leg," he said.

"You will not!" Yvonne exclaimed before Laura could object. But her words didn't keep Eddie from moving his weight to his bad leg and crutches before kicking the ball with his left foot. Because of his awkward angle, the ball went only a couple feet.

"A cripple can't play," Keith Rhodes called as he ran toward them for the ball.

"Ignore him," Laura said. She kicked the ball as hard as she could, and it sailed to the other end of the playground. Good. Keith could chase that silly ball.

"Keith's a creep," Kenny said. "You need practice, that's all. Maybe we can borrow a kickball sometime and work on it."

"Mama says you can learn to walk without crutches. That ought to be first," Laura said.

Eddie immediately handed his crutches to Kenny and took a few wobbly steps. Laura grabbed the crutches and propped him up. He seemed glad for the help.

"It'll just take practice," she said. "Look how fast you learned to walk with crutches."

"I'll put more weight on that leg every day. By the end of the month, I'll be playing kickball."

"Sure you will," Laura said, and she half-believed it. Sometimes she thought his leg would get better, and other days she knew it never would. She still prayed about it because Mama said she should.

The bell rang, calling the students back to the classrooms. Eddie gave Laura a smile and a see-you-later nod as he hobbled into Miss Burch's room.

Mrs. Jamison handed out arithmetic books and assigned a page of twenty problems. A half hour later, she took up the papers and switched the subject to government.

"Because this is an election year, and since our government is in the forefront because of the war, we're going to have an election in our classroom. We'll elect a classroom president to be in charge of our war-stamp program. You will want to elect someone who has leadership skills and is a good organizer. Anyone who wants to run should pick up one of these nomination forms, fill it out, and bring it back to school tomorrow." She held up several small sheets.

Laura glanced at the other students. Which one of the boys would make a good president? She didn't know all the boys in her class, but no outstanding candidate came to mind. She would make a better president. Laura sat up straighter in her desk. Why couldn't a girl be president? She knew how to organize. Hadn't she been keeping good records at the hotel office? Mama had told her last night that she'd like Laura to take a shift at the office after she got home from school.

She started to hold up her hand to ask if a girl could run but thought better of it. She'd ask in private, after school.

The rest of the day passed slowly as Laura waited for her opportunity to get a form. When the last bell rang, she hung back as the other students rushed for the door. As she pretended to search her desk for something, she watched the teacher's desk out of the corner of her eye. Two boys picked up forms. When all of the students were out of the room, she walked to the desk and picked up a form.

"Is this just for boys?" she asked.

"Oh!" Mrs. Jamison said and looked a long moment at Laura. "I guess a girl could run. Sure, why not? But you must be aware that your chances at being elected aren't as good as a boy's."

"I'm a good organizer," Laura said.

"I'm sure you are, but that has nothing to do with it. Students usually vote for boys, but that doesn't mean you won't get any votes. Give it some serious thought, Laura. If you still want to run, turn in your form tomorrow. It would be interesting calling someone 'Madam President.' "

CHAPTER 5

The Elections

"I never heard of a girl president," Eddie said at supper that night.

"Does that mean there can't be one?" Laura asked.

"It sure doesn't," Margie said. "A few years ago no one would have believed I could work at Boeing in production. Now there are lots of women who work on the line."

"But that's because of the war," Gary said. "Pass the potatoes, please."

"Girls are as smart as boys, aren't they, Dad?" Margie asked. Laura was glad she'd waited until suppertime to start this discussion about the class election. She wanted Margie on her side.

"I'm not getting into this kind of argument," Dad said with a grin. "Especially with your mother sitting here."

"If you want to be president, then you should go for it," Margie said. "I don't know if you'd win, but you should run. I'll help you with your campaign speech."

"I don't know if we give speeches," Laura said. "But I could put up a banner like the one we made for Eddie."

"It's all right with me if you're a candidate," Mama said. She looked at Dad. "Any objections?"

"Not as long as she knows that her chances of winning are

slim." He looked at Laura. "I don't want you to be disappointed."

"I won't be. I'm going to win," she said. At his frown, she added, "Maude says to always have a positive attitude. So that's what I'm going to do. Think positive." She handed the nomination form to Gary, who passed it to Ginny, who passed it to Dad. "You have to sign it to indicate that you know the duties of the president include the war-stamp collection."

The next day at school, Laura handed in her completed form.

"Yours is the third one," Mrs. Jamison said. "I gave out three yesterday, so the race is on." She looked over the forms, and when the bell rang, she called the class to order. They said the Lord's Prayer and the Pledge of Allegiance, and then Mrs. Jamison asked Laura, Jay Armstrong, and Keith Rhodes to come to the front of the class.

"These three students are running for president of our class. We'll let them talk to the class tomorrow and answer any questions you may have, and then on Thursday we'll vote on our class president."

"What do we talk about?" Jay asked.

"Why you would make a good class president," Mrs. Jamison said. "You don't have to give a long speech. A couple of minutes will do. You may be seated."

Laura walked to her desk and thought of reasons why she'd make a good president. She jotted her ideas down on paper so she could remember them when she was standing in front of the class tomorrow. Maybe this wasn't such a good idea after all. She'd never spoken to a whole group of kids.

"You'll do great," Yvonne said as they walked home from school.

Eddie had persuaded Mama to let him walk all the way home, so he limped on his crutches beside Kenny. "Are you going to vote for Laura?" he asked. "I would if I were in her class."

Kenny looked sideways at Laura and didn't commit himself. "Our class would be the only one with a girl president."

"We may be the only class with a president. Eddie's class isn't electing one," Laura said.

"Not yet," Yvonne said. "But I asked Miss Burch if we were going to, and she said it might be a good idea."

At the hotel, Kenny waved good-bye and walked on home, but Yvonne climbed the stairs and called her mom to see if she could stay awhile to work on Laura's campaign banner. Mama let Laura get a sheet before she took over office duties.

The girls were cutting out letters in the lobby when the postman came. Eddie sorted the mail.

"You got a letter from Bruce," he said.

Laura put down her scissors and scurried to the desk. "I did? Just me?" Usually Bruce's letters were addressed to the entire family. Only once had she received one addressed specifically to her. It had been a thank-you letter because she had sent him a bookmark she'd made in Sunday school. In carefully scrolled letters, she'd written a portion of the Twenty-third Psalm—the part about walking in the valley of the shadow of death but fearing no evil because God was with him. Bruce was as big a hero in her eyes as her father, but she was afraid for him, and she didn't want him to be afraid.

Eddie handed her the letter and continued sticking letters in boxes.

Laura carefully opened it and scanned the contents. "He's using the code!" she exclaimed. "He wants a piece of pie. I think that means *France*. Eddie, can you get the code sheet from the drawer?" He gave it to her, and she matched words and phrases. "He's written down what he wants for his first meal home. Translation: He was in Italy, then England, then in the D-Day invasion, and now he's in France."

The postmark was a month earlier, but Allied troops were still pushing across Europe toward Germany, so Bruce was exactly where Dad had suspected. Knowing for sure made Laura feel closer to Bruce. She wondered where in France and decided her next letter would have code words for the big towns so she could pinpoint his exact location.

At supper that night, Laura shared the news from Bruce's letter. She also talked about her speech and showed off her banner, which read LAURA EDWARDS FOR PRESIDENT! Her sister Margie said her banner was great and then gave her some pointers on how to speak to the class. Still, Laura had sweaty palms when it was speech time the next day.

"Ladies first," Mrs. Jamison said. Laura hid a frown. Margie had told her to focus on how the candidates would organize and run the stamp drive instead of the boy-girl issue.

Laura walked to the front of the room and began. "My friends and classmates, I would be a good president because I've had experience organizing things. Over the summer I had a real job. I ran a hotel office during the afternoons." She listed her responsibilities. "I would use those skills to organize the war-stamp drives. My brother Bruce is in the army, and I work very hard on the home front to keep him safe. Please vote for me."

The class applauded. Next, Jay spoke. He said he wanted to be president and would appreciate everyone voting for him.

Keith mentioned the importance of war-stamp sales in his speech.

"Any questions?" Mrs. Jamison asked. Laura was prepared for some, but no one raised a hand. "Tomorrow morning we'll have the election. It'll be by secret ballot, just like real elections, so no one will know how you voted. We'll count the ballots in class."

On the playground, when the teacher had walked back into the school, Keith sidled up to Laura. "Isn't your big hotel job in that place where the Japs lived?" He didn't wait for an answer before he said in a loud voice so other kids could hear, "She's running a Jap hotel!"

Laura was momentarily dumbstruck. Sure, the Wakamutsus were of Japanese ancestry, but they weren't the Japanese the United States was fighting.

"Those tenants came here before the war," she said. "They're on the American side."

"Sure they are," Keith said. "That's why the government locked them up."

Laura had no reply to that, but she asked Mama that afternoon when she was taking over the office.

"The Wakamutsus should never have been sent to the relocation center. Most of the Japanese would have become American citizens if they were allowed to. Sachiko, Minoru, and Kiyoshi are Americans, born right here in Seattle."

"Then why were they locked up?" Laura said.

"I can't explain that. I think it was a big mistake made by people who are afraid of someone who looks different."

Laura nodded but didn't really understand.

The next morning at school, Laura hung her banner at the front of the room. Neither one of the other candidates had made a sign.

"Are there any questions for the candidates before we vote?" Mrs. Jamison asked. She wrote the three names on the blackboard, and each student voted for one on a small piece of paper. Laura voted for herself. Dad had said if she didn't have the confidence in her ability to lead, then she shouldn't be a candidate.

Mrs. Jamison carried a large jar down the aisles, and students dropped their ballots in it. She carefully mixed them up as if for a drawing, then she pulled one out at a time and read the name. With each name drawn, she put a tally mark by that candidate's name on the blackboard.

Laura held her breath as each name was read. She had won before the last few names were drawn. Of the thirty-two votes in her class, she already had eighteen before the final votes were read. That was more than half the class. Jay ended up with seven, Keith had four, and Laura had twenty-one votes.

"Madam President, would you take over the meeting of the class?" Mrs. Jamison asked.

Laura walked carefully to the front of the room. Her heart felt as if it would burst inside her, and happiness washed over her. She had actually won—and by a landslide. What a feeling!

She and Yvonne had planned what she would say if she won or lost. Now she tried to remember. She should have brought her notes to the front with her.

"Thank you for electing me president. I'll do my best to do a good job. The first thing I'd like our class to do is make a banner for our room. We can use this sheet for the backing." She pointed to her campaign banner. "Would each one of you draw something that represents you or anything about you and sign it? We'll put the drawings on the banner."

"That's a fine idea, Laura," Mrs. Jamison said. She turned to the class. "Why don't you think about what you will draw, and after arithmetic and reading, we'll make the banner."

At recess, Laura ran outside and told the others of her big win. "We're making the banner, just like we planned," Laura told Yvonne. It had actually been Margie's idea. She said it would unite the class, and Yvonne and Laura thought it was a wonderful plan.

When Mrs. Jamison let them draw their objects for the banner, Laura drew a picture of the office at the hotel. She'd based her campaign on her experience there, so she thought it was fitting. Jay drew a bicycle, since he rode everywhere. Keith drew a face with slanted eyes and big buck teeth, like in a newspaper cartoon, and then made a big *X* over it to show that the Japanese should be eliminated. Another student drew an airplane dropping bombs because his brother was a pilot. Still another drawing was of the American flag.

Each student pinned a drawing on the sheet until everyone was represented. Some of the drawings were not war-related. A teddy bear, a baseball bat, a birthday cake, and a kickball found places on the banner.

Before they left school, Laura and Kenny hung the banner above the door. Laura couldn't wait for next week's class meeting, when the war stamps would be sold.

Eddie's class was also going to hold an election. Laura urged him to run for president.

"Do you think they'd elect a cripple?" he asked. That was the first time Laura had heard Eddie call himself that, and she hoped it was the last time.

"You have one weak leg," she said. "And it's getting better." She'd been helping him with exercises to strengthen it. Again they used the hotel hallways as practice areas, and he'd lengthened his walk each day. "I didn't think it would work again, but you've forced it to. You may have to wear the brace, but you won't need crutches much longer."

"But I'll always have a limp."

"What about President Roosevelt? He had polio, and he's the leader of our country. And I think he'll be elected again. Who could beat him?" She'd heard Dad say that just the night before.

With a little more persuasion, Eddie was convinced to run. Laura declared herself his campaign manager. Since he was helping in the office after school, he could use that job as a qualification in his speech. Yvonne and Kenny helped them make a banner that read VOTE FOR EDDIE.

On the day of his class campaign speeches, Eddie walked to the front of his classroom without his crutches. Laura wished she'd been there to see him, but Yvonne filled her in on every detail. When it was time for questions, Yvonne stood up and talked about how Eddie had worked hard to overcome polio and that he was a determined boy who would work hard for their class. Everyone applauded when she sat down.

The vote was between Eddie and one other boy, and although it was a close race, Eddie was elected president.

"The Edwards siblings," Laura said at recess when she'd been told of Eddie's victory. "What a team!"

Laura and Eddie fell into a routine. They worked together in the office after school, putting up the mail and giving it out. When there was no activity at the office, they did their homework. They planned their class meetings together, and Laura was very thankful that they were in different classrooms so they could both be presidents. She liked being in charge, and so did Eddie.

They continued Eddie's exercises, and he used his crutches less and less. One evening in September, he put away his crutches for good. Laura thought they ought to burn the crutches as a symbol of Eddie's triumph, but Mama said they'd better keep them. Mama splurged and bought a roast for dinner with meat stamps she'd been saving and said it would be a good-bye-to-crutches dinner. She invited Maude to join the family. They were in a celebratory mood, but when Dad came home things changed.

"What's wrong?" Laura asked when she saw his grim expression.

"Bad news," he said. "Phil Johnson died." Laura had to search her memory until she remembered the name. Phil Johnson was president of Boeing, but he wasn't an old man.

"I didn't know he was sick," she said.

"He didn't know he was, either. He was in Wichita to check on the facility where they're making B-29s when a tumor in his brain started bleeding. It was all very sudden."

"What will happen at the plant?" Mama asked.

"I don't know who will move into his position. Work buzzed with speculation, but the outcome was that his death shouldn't change anything. Phil would have expected us to keep production going, but it won't be the same without him around."

The good-bye-to-crutches dinner became a good-bye-to-Phil

Johnson dinner. Margie had only met him once, but she told the story of shaking his hand when he came to the line. Dad remembered him as an intelligent man of vision.

"If there's one thing this war has taught us, it's how to deal with death," Maude said. "We just give our dead to the Lord and somehow keep going."

Laura thought of Yvonne's brother and how hard it had been on the Dreger family to let him go. She thought of Neil Palmer and how Corrine still hadn't given up hope of his return. *How will it all end?* she wondered. *And when will it all end?*

As the days of fall slipped by, Laura followed the campaign for president of the United States. She listened to President Roosevelt's speeches and heard some of New York Governor Dewey's radio talks, too. She didn't have a doubt that Mr. Roosevelt would be reelected. He was president when she was born, and he was still president.

"He can't be too confident," Maude said one day when she was picking up her mail. "Of course the Republicans are against him, but there are even some Democrats who think he's been president too long. Whoever heard of a man being elected to four terms? Of course, I'd hate to have a change of leadership in the middle of the war."

"He'll be elected," Laura said with confidence. She liked politics, she liked the people voting, and she liked President Roosevelt. Because he and Eddie had both had polio, she lumped them together in her mind.

She celebrated when election results were in and President Roosevelt was declared the winner. "He can lead us through the war," Laura said. "Maybe he'll even run a fifth time."

CHAPTER 6

The Battle of the Bulge

"Jerry's on Guam," Maude said on Christmas Eve afternoon. She stood at the office window and read her son's letter out loud. When she finished, she folded the letter and held it to her heart. "Laura, let me look at that atlas again."

Laura was glad she'd carried the atlas to the office that afternoon. They'd been looking at it last night in their apartment after the latest news report on the Battle of the Bulge. The Germans had pushed the Allied front back sixty miles, and the American death count was very high.

Once again fear held a desperate grip on Laura's heart. Was Bruce there? Was he okay? She knew he'd been in France earlier, and it seemed logical that he would be moving on toward Germany. Last night, Dad had pointed on the map to the town of Bastogne in Belgium.

When the Germans had demanded the surrender of the town, General McAuliffe had replied, "Nuts." Dad had said that was a gutsy thing to do, but the last news was that the town was still under siege. Was Bruce holed up there? Or was he marching toward the town to fight?

She had carried the atlas to the office so she could look at the map again. Now she opened it to the Pacific Islands and located

Guam. "They must have sandy beaches and coconuts there," Laura said. What a contrast to the intense cold and snow that the reporter from Europe had mentioned in his live report on the radio last night.

"I wish we had developed more to that code," Maude said. "Then I could know what Jerry was doing. He mentioned nuts and bolts and the sound of the airplane engines. Maybe that's a clue."

"Maybe he works on airplanes," Laura said. "Or maybe he rides in them and drops bombs." She had a sudden image in her mind of Japanese people on the ground running from falling buildings. She shuddered and moved her finger on the map from Guam to the Philippines, where Corrine's boyfriend had last been heard from.

"I'm sick of this war!" she exclaimed. She was stunned by her own words. They had boiled up from her heart and come out of her mouth before she could think about them. "That's not patriotic, is it?" Laura asked. "I shouldn't have said that."

"I'm sick of it, too," Maude said. "It has nothing to do with patriotism. It has to do with Christmas and peace on earth, and that's not what we're experiencing, is it?"

"No," Laura said simply. She looked at the Christmas tree in the lobby. She and Eddie had decorated it with their ornaments and ones the Wakamutsus had left behind. The star at the top glistened, and colorful glass ball decorations hung from green branches. Bruce didn't have a Christmas tree. He was probably in that dark European forest the radio news correspondent had described, shivering with the cold and wanting to be home for Christmas.

Maude had turned to stare at the tree, too. "I guess Jerry's Christmas tree will be a palm tree. I doubt the army decorates barracks for holidays."

"No, I don't think soldiers have time to put up real Christmas trees," Laura said.

With a forced note of cheerfulness in her voice, Maude said, "We miss them, but life goes on. Is everything ready for the party tonight?"

"I think so. Eddie and Gary are going to move tables out here around five. Mama didn't want to block the hallways too soon, but she wants everything set up before Dad gets home."

The party had been Laura's idea, and now she wished she'd never had it. Should they celebrate at home when friends and family couldn't be there?

"Laura, this is Christmas Eve. We have to get in a festive spirit," Maude said.

"How can we when. . . ?" Her voice trailed off.

"It's time you faced your fear. What's the worst that can happen to them?" Maude asked in a quiet voice.

"They could be killed."

"And then what?"

"We get the telegram that tells us they're dead."

"Yes, but what would happen to Bruce and Jerry and the others?"

"They'd go to heaven."

"Exactly. That wouldn't be bad for them, now would it?"

Laura studied Maude's eyes. In them she saw serenity and acceptance. Not the fear that was always in her own eyes.

"But what if they're tortured or die in terrible agony?"

"We pray that God will be with them." Maude reached inside the office window and took Laura's hand. "You are too young to know all this fear. It doesn't help them. It only harms you. Now, give your fear to God, and He'll deal with it."

Laura closed her eyes and prayed that God would take her fear away. She opened her eyes and felt peace settle on her.

"Better?" Maude said.

"Yes. Better," Laura answered.

"Good. Whenever you feel overwhelmed by fear, ask God to take it from you."

"How come you're so smart, Maude?"

She smiled. "Because I lived with fear too long. I'm going to find your mother and see if she needs help."

The party was for everyone in the hotel. At seven, each person was to bring his or her own plate and silverware and one dish to share with the others. Mr. Benedetto from apartment 10 was going to bring his phonograph and some records. He mostly had classical, but Maude had some Christmas albums she was going to bring, and Ginny had said she was going to guard her new Frank Sinatra record with her life and make sure it was played over and over.

The boys set up the tables early, confiscating as many as they could from residents in nearby rooms. Every room in the hotel was filled, but some people couldn't come to the party because of family gatherings and work shifts. Those who could make it wandered into the narrow lobby before the party officially began at seven.

Dad led the group in a prayer for the servicemen and in celebration for the birthday of Jesus. Then the merriment began. At least fifty people filled the narrow space, and all seemed to be talking at once. Even Mrs. Lind, carrying dozens of cookies, came to the dinner party.

"I've been saving my sugar rations," she said, "so I could make my traditional Christmas favorites." She pointed to each kind. "These are date pinwheels. These white ones are Mexican wedding cakes, and these are my favorite—gingersnaps."

Laura put two cookies on her plate before she headed to the main food table loaded with chicken, potatoes cooked in a variety of ways, and lots of dishes of green beans.

Mr. Arnold struck up a conversation with Laura about his latest letter from his grandson. Because he had also used Laura's code, he knew that Dale was in Belgium.

"He may be in that awful Battle of the Bulge right now," Mr. Arnold said.

"Then may God be with him," Laura said and felt peace by saying it.

He nodded. "Yes, may God be with him."

Although several people lingered in the lobby talking, most had gone back to their own rooms by nine o'clock. Laura's brothers returned tables to their proper owners, and the girls picked up and swept and scrubbed the lobby. The entire area was cleaned up long before it was time to leave for the midnight church service, and the air of goodwill and cheer stayed with Laura.

The church was decorated in evergreen boughs and red bows. At the front sat a manger with real people representing the characters in the Christmas story. A tiny infant played the part of the baby Jesus. This year the baby slept through the whole performance and didn't cry once. Laura prayed for victory in Europe and in the Pacific, and for peace all over the world.

When the Edwardses returned to the hotel, they opened Christmas presents, which wasn't their tradition, but since Dad and Margie had to be at work on Christmas morning, it seemed the best thing to do.

Along with a pocket-sized atlas and a sweater, Laura received a wooden gavel from Dad, who said he was sorry he'd ever doubted that she would be elected president. She went to bed tired, happy, and at peace for the first time in a long time.

The next day didn't seem like Christmas since Dad and Margie were off to work before Laura got up. She and Eddie did their morning hotel chores, and that afternoon she again sat at the office while Mama worked on a Christmas feast for supper.

During the next week, news from the European front filled the papers. "What do you think of Patton's army entering Bastogne?" Mr. Arnold asked Laura one afternoon. "Pretty good, eh?"

Laura agreed and listened to his opinion of the Battle of the Bulge. Whenever fear edged into her mind, she forced it out by asking God to take it. The fear came less often, and she was able to talk about the battles and not worry that Bruce might be fighting in them.

Just after the first of the year, Laura and Eddie were working in the office when a telegram came for Mr. Arnold. A deep foreboding enveloped Laura as she directed the delivery boy to Mr. Arnold's room.

"I'm going with him," Laura said. There had been too many stories told at school for her to think that a telegram meant anything but bad news.

She stood in the hallway and waited for Mr. Arnold to answer the messenger's knock. As soon as he saw the boy's telegraph uniform, Mr. Arnold's face turned a sickly white. He signed on the clipboard with a shaking hand and took the telegram. He was shutting the door when he looked up and met Laura's gaze.

"Come in," he said in a very low voice. He handed her the telegram. "Open this, please. My hands aren't steady."

Laura carefully opened the envelope. The message was as she suspected, except it was from Mr. Arnold's daughter and not the army.

"Sit down," she said. Instead of reading it aloud, she held it so he could see it.

His hand flew to his heart, and a groan escaped his lips. "No. . . no. . .no."

Laura found a glass and filled it with water. "Drink this, Mr. Arnold. I'm going to get my mother."

She hated to leave him, but she didn't know how to help him. With wings on her feet, she ran down the long hallway, around the corner, and down another hallway to the apartment.

"Mama! Mama!" she called as she opened the door. "Come quick. It's Mr. Arnold's grandson."

"Dale's here?" Mama asked.

"No! Dale's been killed. Mr. Arnold needs you."

Mama dropped her mending and followed Laura back down the hallways to Mr. Arnold's room. He sat exactly where he had been when Laura had left him, only now his head was bowed and tears dripped onto his white shirt.

"I'm so sorry," Mama said. She picked up the telegram and read it. "Let's call your daughter from the office phone. She'll want to know that you received the news about Dale and that you're with friends. She'll need your support, Mr. Arnold."

Laura carried Mr. Arnold's address book and held on to his arm as he walked between her and Mama down the hall.

"What's all the. . . ?" Mrs. Lind had opened her door, looked at them, and then said, "Dale?"

Laura nodded, and Mrs. Lind backed into her room and shut the door.

By the time Eddie had moved out of the way and Mama had Mr. Arnold seated in the office chair, Mrs. Lind stood at the office window, holding out a cup of hot tea.

"I already gave him water," Laura said.

"He needs a good strong cup of tea," Mrs. Lind said and handed the cup through the window. Mr. Arnold took a sip, then drained the cup and took a deep breath. His color looked a little better.

Laura held Mr. Arnold's hand, or rather he held hers, in a tight grip. Mama talked to the operator and gave the number for the long-distance call.

As soon as she had Dale's mother on the line, Mama handed the phone to Mr. Arnold.

"Let's give him some privacy, kids," Mama said. Eddie and Laura edged around Mr. Arnold in the close quarters and followed Mama out the office door.

"The poor man," Mrs. Lind said. "He thought the sun rose and set on that grandson of his."

"Dale was always good about writing Mr. Arnold," Mama said. "I wonder where he was killed."

"Mrs. Edwards?" Mr. Arnold called from the office. Mama went inside while Laura and Eddie sat on the lobby couch by Mrs. Lind. A few minutes later Mama and Mr. Arnold came out of the office.

"Laura, will you take Mr. Arnold back to his room?" Mama asked. "I have some calls to make."

Laura and Eddie escorted Mr. Arnold down the hall, with Mrs. Lind leading the way. Once he was propped in his favorite upholstered chair, Mr. Arnold told them about Dale, who had been killed on December 17—the second day of the Battle of the Bulge. "And we're just now finding out," he said. "He's been gone nearly two weeks, and we're just now finding out."

"Dale's a war hero," Eddie said.

"Yes, he is. He is," Mr. Arnold said.

They shared memories about Dale, although Laura and Eddie had never met him. Laura looked at the framed photograph of Dale that Mrs. Lind held and remembered the stories Mr. Arnold had told her about this special young man.

A knock sounded on the door. Laura answered it and ushered Mama and Maude inside.

"Your train leaves in two hours," Mama said. "Your daughter will pick you up in Albuquerque tomorrow afternoon. We'll help him get around, kids, so you can go back to the office."

Supper was delayed while Mama and Maude took Mr. Arnold to the train station. "I hated leaving him alone on the train," Mama said. "But the conductor was looking after him. He needs to be with family."

"Did Mr. Arnold have the money for a trip?" Laura asked. From time to time he'd let slip that money was tight.

Mama glanced at Dad before she said, "Sometimes others step in when a friend needs help. Mr. Arnold needed to be with his family."

"I'm glad you helped him," Laura said. That night before she went to bed, she asked God to help Mr. Arnold, and she thanked Him that they hadn't received a telegram about Bruce.

CHAPTER 7

The Wakamutsus Return

Eddie's limp was barely noticeable as he, Kenny, Yvonne, and Laura walked home from school on a damp January afternoon. Their discussion centered on the war-stamp sales, which were going well.

"At the end of the month, we'll do another count," Laura said. Her room and Eddie's room were both in the blue ribbon group on the sales chart. "My room may take over the lead by itself."

"Maybe, maybe not," Yvonne said. "Our room has a new plan to get more sales."

Laura raised her eyebrows. Eddie hadn't said anything about it, and he eventually told her everything, even if he tried to keep a secret.

They arrived at the hotel, and the group split up. As Laura and Eddie climbed up to the lobby, she asked him about the new plan.

Eddie didn't answer. Instead he stared at the office.

"Eddie?" Laura turned to look at what had him so fascinated, and her mouth dropped open in shock.

Mama and a Japanese woman stood in the office. It had been nearly three years since Laura had seen her, but the woman had to be Mrs. Wakamutsu.

Laura hesitantly approached the office. Eddie seemed just as stunned as she was, for he hung back behind her.

A Jap in the office. A Jap. The word *Jap* kept echoing in Laura's mind. What would Yvonne say? Oh, her friend had known that a Japanese family had lived there before the war, but somehow that knowledge and seeing a real Jap didn't fit together.

"Kids, come say hello," Mama said.

Laura and Eddie edged forward.

"Hello, little ones. My, how you've grown since I last saw you," Mrs. Wakamutsu said. "We've brought a surprise for you."

Can there be more of a surprise? Laura wondered. She finally found her voice and said hello. "When did you arrive?"

"We got here this morning, sooner than we expected. I wrote your mother, but we arrived before my letter." She laughed, a quiet sound. "We are so happy to be back home."

Home? Home! Where would they stay? There were no vacancies at the hotel.

"We've rearranged things a bit," Mama said. "You girls are all in one room now. It's wall to wall with five beds, but it will work for the time being."

Laura gazed silently at her mother. Five beds. She, Corrine, Margie, and Ginny made four, and there was only one set of bunks in that room. Laura was quite sure the Wakamutsus' only daughter had left the relocation center in the summer when she'd found a sponsor and a job in Chicago. Ginny had read that letter to her. Well, Sachiko must have come back for a visit now that the Wakamutsus were free.

"Eddie, we've put Minoru and Kiyoshi in with you and Gary. Mr. and Mrs. Wakamutsu will use the room Corrine and Margie shared." Mama turned to Mrs. Wakamutsu and hugged her. "I'm so delighted you're back."

"Do you want us to put up the mail?" Laura asked. Their normal routine was to put up their school things, get a glass of milk and a piece of bread, and report back to the office to relieve Mama before mail time.

"Sure," Mama said. "We've still got lots to do to get everyone settled in. Get a snack, and then you can take over." Laura turned to walk to the apartment when her mother called her back. "Oh, wait, the surprise!" Mama scurried out of the office and walked with Laura and Eddie down the hall.

The apartment was no longer a haven of peace and family love. Boxes were so stacked in the middle of the living room, there was barely room to walk. Two Japanese boys were carrying boxes toward the bedrooms under the direction of Mr. Wakamutsu. Laura knew they had to be Minoru and Kiyoshi, but they had grown a foot taller since she'd last seen them.

Laura and Eddie exchanged greetings with the boys, and Mama called, "Miyoko!"

A young Japanese girl about Laura's size walked into the living room from the direction of the girls' bedroom.

"Here's the surprise," Mama said. "Miyoko Ito is staying with the Wakamutsus for a while. She'll be going to your school. Too bad she won't be in your class. She's a grade younger."

Laura stared at the Japanese girl until Mama nudged her.

"Hello," Laura managed.

Miyoko made a small bow in graceful Japanese fashion. "I'm so pleased to meet you," she said.

"You can introduce her around at school tomorrow," Mama said.

What was Mama thinking? Take a Jap to school? Be friends with a Jap? What would the other kids think? Oh, what about Yvonne?

"I'd better go back to the office," Laura said. "It's almost mail time."

"Miyoko, would you like to join them in the office?" Mama asked.

Miyoko looked at Laura and said, "Perhaps in a little while. I am still unpacking."

"Of course," Mama said.

Laura skipped her usual after-school snack and hurried back to the office, carrying her schoolwork with her.

"You may go back to the apartment if you wish," she told the Japanese woman at the office. "Miyoko is still unpacking."

"Yes, we have lots to do," Mrs. Wakamutsu said. "We are storing some boxes in the linen room. How could we have accumulated so much during our stay at the relocation center?"

Laura smiled but didn't comment.

"Laura, I hope you will be kind to Miyoko. Her mother died two years ago, and her father is in the army. He has entrusted her to our care until he returns. If he returns."

Laura nodded but didn't promise anything. Mrs. Wakamutsu left the office, and Laura sat down with a sigh of relief. What was happening to her world? Just when she had gotten settled, something else happened to disrupt her life.

Eddie opened the office door.

"What do you think?" Laura asked without explaining any further.

"I'm glad she's not a boy. You get to take her around school and not me. Why is she here?"

Laura explained the little she knew about Miyoko. "I feel sorry for her, but she's a Jap."

It felt odd to say that out loud. It felt wrong, yet kids at school said it all the time. *"Get the Japs." "Kill the Japs."*

"Mail here yet?" Mrs. Lind was at the window as was her habit this time of day.

"He's running a little late," Laura said. She held out the newspaper. "The Wakamutsus are back."

"I know. I saw them move in this morning." She shrugged. "It's nothing to me. I've rented with them, but I've heard talk that some of the new residents. . .aren't pleased." She said the last as if she were searching for the right words. "After all, if Roosevelt thought they were a threat and had them locked up, aren't they still a threat? That's what I've heard people say." She lumbered over to the couch and sat down with the paper.

Mrs. Lind had a point. Laura didn't know much about the lock-up order, but she was going to ask questions. But who could she ask? She might not get any time alone with Mama and Dad without the Japs around.

There it was again. It didn't feel right thinking of the Wakamutsus as Japs. She had thought of them as the Japanese family her parents knew. But talk at school was about Japs in America being spies. That's why they had been sent to the relocation centers and internment camps.

The mailman delivered a large packet of letters. Eddie took half, and Laura took half.

"Here's a letter from Mr. Arnold," Eddie said. "It's to Mama and Dad. And here's the one from the Wakamutsus."

"Nothing from Bruce in my pile," Laura said.

"Nothing here, either," Eddie said. "But here's a letter from Jerry Bowers."

Of course, Maude—that's who she could ask about the Japs. Laura could ask her anything. "I'll deliver it. Can you take care of the office by yourself?"

Eddie looked at her with his who-do-you-think-you're-talking-to look.

"Sorry. I'll be back in a few minutes."

Laura scurried down the hall to Maude's apartment. Once inside, she impatiently waited while Maude read her son's letter before bombarding her with questions.

"He was still on Guam when he wrote this," Maude reported. "I wonder if he went to the Philippines. There was bad fighting in Luzon."

"It doesn't do any good to worry about him," Laura said. "Face your fear. What's the worst that could happen?"

Maude smiled. "Didn't I give you this lecture?"

"Yes, and it helped me."

"And it helps me when fear rears its ugly head," Maude said. "What's bothering you now? You've got that look." She reached over and smoothed the line between Laura's eyebrows. "If you scrunch up like that whenever you have a problem, you're going to have some big wrinkles."

Laura moved over by the mirror beside the door and looked at her reflection. Sure enough, she had a scrunched-up look. "Eddie looks like this when he's worried."

"Sometimes siblings do that. They can have some of the same habits. So what's bothering you?"

Laura walked back to a chair across from Maude and announced,

"The Wakamutsus are back."

"I know."

"They're Japs."

"Yes, they are."

Didn't Maude understand? "Jerry's fighting the Japs. Doesn't that bother you? Don't you hate them?"

"We're not fighting the Wakamutsus. They've lived here for many years. Their children were born in Seattle. That makes them American citizens."

"Then why were they sent to relocation centers?"

Maude pursed her lips. "That's a good question, and I don't have a good answer because I don't understand it myself."

"Didn't President Roosevelt send them to the centers?"

"He signed the order, but I imagine there was a lot of pressure brought on him by people who were afraid. See, Laura, fear makes people do some crazy things." Maude explained about the removal of the Japanese to the inland relocation centers and the new order letting them return to coastal cities like Seattle.

"Couldn't they prove they weren't spies?"

"I don't think they were given the chance. The thought was that most of them have relatives in Japan. They would have to have divided loyalties. You ought to talk to Mrs. Wakamutsu about this."

"I can't ask her!"

"Why not? I imagine she'd be very interested in your reaction. She's going to get it a lot. People are still fearful. They act badly when they're afraid. In fact, Mr. Wakamutsu may have a hard time finding someone to give him a job."

"The Wakamutsus brought a Japanese girl with them. I have to take her to school tomorrow."

"Oh, so that's what all this is about."

"All the kids hate the Japs."

"So tomorrow could be a hard day."

"Very hard."

"You're the only girl president in the school, Laura. You're a leader. You can figure out a way to make the students accept this girl."

"How?"

Maude smiled again, a sly smile. "I don't know, but you're a bright girl. You'll figure it out."

That wasn't the answer Laura wanted, and she muttered to herself as she walked down the hall to the office. How would she handle tomorrow? What would Yvonne do when she met Miyoko?

That evening the Edwardses and the Wakamutsus had a grand dinner. There wasn't room for everyone at the dinner table, so the younger kids carried their plates to the living room to eat. An air of festivity dominated the small apartment. Laura tried to get into the mood, but she felt as if a cloud the size of the one that normally blocked the top of Mount Rainier hung over her.

Miyoko asked Laura some questions about school, and Laura answered them the best she could.

"You'll have to go to the principal's office, and she'll tell you which class you'll be in. Mrs. Sawyer's class is one of the smallest, so I think you'll end up there." That class was always at the bottom of the stamp-sale list because it didn't have as many kids to buy stamps.

As soon as everyone had eaten, the two families crowded into the living room for a meeting. Every chair was taken, and the floor was covered with kids, some sitting on unopened boxes.

"You all know the sleeping arrangements," Dad said. "As soon as there are vacancies in the hotel, we'll spread out. But for now this will have to do. We had a letter from Mr. Arnold today." Dad explained to the Wakamutsus that Dale had been killed in the war. "He's going to move in with his daughter in New Mexico. We'll crate up his things and ship them to him. As soon as that's done, there will be one hotel room available to us. Any questions?"

"Can we do our homework in the office?" Eddie asked.

"That shouldn't be a problem," Mama said.

That was a relief. Doing homework in the office had to be much better than coming to this cramped apartment to find a space to sit down. Maybe when they were moved to other hotel rooms, things would get better.

"Any other questions?" Dad waited, but no one spoke up. "Then I'd like us all to bow our heads to thank God for the Wakamutsus' return."

Dad ended his prayer with the usual request that the war would soon end and that Bruce, Neil, Jerry, and the other soldiers would return home. This time he included Leonard Ito, Miyoko's father, in his prayer.

The bedroom was crowded, and it took Laura awhile to get to sleep on the hard cot. Miyoko's cot was only inches from hers. Before sleep claimed her, the thought crossed Laura's mind that the little Jap could try to hurt her while she slept. She pushed the thought away. There was that ugly fear again. Miyoko was an American. Her father was fighting in the war. Surely that would overrule her Japanese blood. For just a moment, she wondered if Miyoko had the same kinds of fears, what with going to a new school and feeling everyone's hatred toward the Japanese.

The next morning, Laura trudged alongside Miyoko as they walked to school. Eddie had left early to set up a special stamp-sale exhibit, the new plan Yvonne had mentioned the day before. Laura figured he didn't want to be seen with Miyoko.

Laura took Miyoko to the office and waited as Mama had told her to while Miyoko was assigned a teacher. Then Laura walked her to her classroom and introduced her to Mrs. Sawyer. At recess, she saw Miyoko standing by herself on the playground and forced herself to go over to her.

"Come meet my friend," Laura said and took Miyoko to where Yvonne was talking with another girl.

"Yvonne, this is Miyoko Ito. She's living with us at the hotel."

Yvonne took one look at Miyoko, glared at Laura, then turned and stormed off.

CHAPTER 8

Miyoko's Story

Laura was ignored by Yvonne the entire day. When it was time to go home, Yvonne didn't walk out of Miss Burch's classroom with Eddie.

"Where's Yvonne?" Laura asked.

"She said she had something to do after school," Eddie said and nodded back at the room.

Laura stuck her head in his classroom and saw Yvonne standing by her desk as if waiting for something. "Coming?"

"No. Traitor!"

Laura recoiled as if she'd been hit. How could Yvonne call her a traitor? She couldn't help it that President Roosevelt had let the Japs out of the relocation centers. Well, if that's the way Yvonne wanted it, fine.

Laura marched back to where Eddie had been joined by Miyoko. "Let's go. Where's Kenny?"

"He went with Jack Heaton," Eddie said.

"Oh," Laura said. So Eddie was also being treated badly because of Miyoko. "Well, let's get home."

"Your friends are not kind," Miyoko said once they were on the sidewalk.

"They don't understand," Eddie said. "We've been at war against the Japs a long time."

"I am not a Jap. I am an American." Miyoko said it with quiet authority that made her seem old. "I was born in California. My father is *Nisei*, born in California. My grandfather was *Issei*, born in Japan, but that was a long time ago. Long before the war."

"But you look Japanese," Laura said.

"That is my heritage, but Japan is not my country." Miyoko said it with such sincerity that Laura believed her.

"It will be hard to convince the kids at school about that," Eddie said.

"I know," Miyoko said. "They call me a Jap, but I am not the enemy. They need to know me, not just the way I look."

They had arrived at the hotel, but Laura held back from climbing the stairs. It would be hard to talk frankly with Mama and Mrs. Wakamutsu around, and Laura wanted to know more about Miyoko. The girl fascinated her in an odd way.

"We want to know you, but it's hard to look past your yellow skin and slanted eyes," Laura said honestly.

"Then I feel sorry for you," Miyoko said. "You are blind."

First she'd been called a traitor by Yvonne, and now Miyoko had called her blind. They were both wrong.

Laura stomped up the stairs. She rushed to the apartment that looked even worse than yesterday. Boxes were opened and half unpacked. Laura glanced at the table where her great-great-grandmother's wooden clock had set. It was gone, and in its place stood a gnarled miniature tree, maybe a foot tall, in a flat green planter. It looked like it belonged in an enchanted forest with its thick trunk and spreading branches.

"Where's the clock?" Laura asked no one in particular, although Kiyoshi, Gary, and Ginny were in the living room. They'd obviously just returned from school, too.

"I don't know," Ginny said. "What is this beautiful tree?"

"Bonsai," Kiyoshi said. "It is Miyoko's. Her father inherited it from his grandfather, who inherited it from his father and his father before him. It is very old."

"Then it is Miyoko's father's tree," Laura said.

"Yes, but he is at war." Then Kiyoshi added matter-of-factly, "He will not return."

"Why not? Is he missing in action?" Laura knew in her heart that Neil Palmer wouldn't return, but he had not been officially declared dead—just missing in action because the navy didn't know what had happened to him.

"No. But when a soldier goes off to war, he does not expect to return."

"Yes, he does," Laura said. "Bruce is coming back."

Kiyoshi shrugged. "A soldier fights to his death. It is the honorable thing to do."

Laura had no reply. She got a drink and then went to the office to relieve her mother and Mrs. Wakamutsu, who were in the office.

"We need to work here a bit longer," Mama said. "Then I must make a few more calls for the March of Dimes. Why don't you and Miyoko walk down to the drugstore and get something special to drink? You can show her the neighborhood." She handed Laura some change. "Laura, I'd like you to be kind to Miyoko. She needs a friend."

Laura nodded. Now what could she do? She went in search of Miyoko and found her in the girls' bedroom. She sat primly on her cot holding Shadow, Sachiko's cat that Margie had adopted when the Wakamutsus were forced to leave for the relocation center. Miyoko petted it with loving strokes.

"Mama says we should walk to the drugstore."

"You do not have to," Miyoko said.

"Yes, I do. Mama said to."

"Of course, you must honor your mother's wishes." Miyoko nudged the cat off her lap, then slipped on her shoes. Laura led the way out of the hotel.

"You have to stay away from the burlesque house. It's not a nice place." Laura pointed out the obvious sites as they walked down the street: the café, the barbershop. Two blocks farther down the street was the drugstore. Laura held the door for Miyoko.

"After you," Miyoko said in that cultured tone of hers.

"Go on. I've got the door," Laura said.

"Thank you," Miyoko said with a nod of her head.

They sat at a small table next to the window and each ordered a Coca-Cola. It was a treat for Laura to be there, but the odd looks she was getting from other customers because of Miyoko took the shine off the special feeling of being independent.

"I'm sorry I said you were blind," Miyoko said.

"That's okay," Laura said. "I'm not blind. I'm not a traitor, either."

"I did not say you were."

"No, but Yvonne did."

They drank their Cokes without talking until Laura couldn't stand the silence. "So what was it like in the relocation center?"

"It was like a town, except we lived in large barracks. My family had one small room next to the Wakamutsus' room. Outside was dusty and so cold in the winter. We had to walk to a big hall to eat bad-tasting food."

"What did you do all day?"

"I went to school. Like here, except we were all yellow-skinned, not white. No one pointed at me and called me a Jap."

"When did your mother die?" It came out more abruptly than Laura intended, but she wanted to get Miyoko off the subject of how she'd been treated at her first day of school in Seattle.

"Over two years ago. November 30, 1942."

"She died in the camp?"

"Yes. She had pneumonia. She was very pretty, even at the end."

"Where is she buried?"

"In Wyoming. We had to leave her there." Tears glistened in Miyoko's eyes. Laura searched for another subject.

"What about your father?"

Miyoko sniffed. "He's in the 442nd. Have you read about them in the paper?"

"No."

"There are many clippings about the bravery of the Nisei Combat Team. I will show them to you. My father is a brave soldier."

If Miyoko's father was a soldier, didn't that prove that he was a loyal American? Laura would get those clippings and show them to Yvonne. Miyoko's family wasn't her brother's enemy. Miyoko's family was fighting to avenge Yvonne's brother's death. Once Yvonne understood that, surely they would be friends again.

"Do you like Frank Sinatra?" Laura asked, changing the subject once again, this time to a neutral topic. "My sister is crazy about his music."

"I have heard him on the radio," Miyoko said. "He sounds nice, but I am not crazy for him."

"Me, either," Laura said. "Hey, did you see the movie *Bataan*?

My sister's boyfriend was on the Philippines when it was taken by the. . ." She'd started to say *Japs* but corrected herself. Even though Miyoko wasn't one of them, she was still of Japanese descent. "Anyway, Corrine has seen that movie five times and cried through it every time."

"I would like to go to the movies," Miyoko said.

"Sometimes Eddie and Kenny and Yvonne and I go on Saturday afternoons. *Meet Me in St. Louis* is playing now. I'll ask Mama if we can go this Saturday." And before then, Laura determined that she'd explain everything to Yvonne.

The girls left the drugstore and walked back by a different route so Miyoko could learn more of the neighborhood.

The next day during school, Yvonne again ignored Laura. It rained during recess, so everyone stayed in classrooms for games instead of going outside. Laura saw Yvonne only once, and that was when Laura and Eddie went from room to room to tell about the March of Dimes drive. The principal had selected them to announce the campaign against polio because of Eddie's brush with the disease. Yvonne didn't even look at Laura when Laura read to the class the information about mothers collecting dimes for polio research.

Eddie talked briefly about having polio and said that he was one of the lucky ones. Many others in the hospitals were in wheelchairs or would always walk with crutches or had died. Laura was surprised when Eddie lifted his pant leg to show his brace. Some of the boys had ridiculed him about it when school had first started, but now it was like a battle wound. He had survived polio. He was a hero.

In her short speech, Laura said that polio research needed to be done right away so that someone else in school didn't get the disease next summer. She saw fear in the eyes of some students and thought that Maude would approve of that fear if it got more dimes in the bucket for research.

After school, Yvonne had left the building before Laura made it to Eddie's room.

Laura and Eddie put the mail up after school, but Mama needed the office phone for last-minute calls about the March of Dimes, so she took over. The whole month of January was March of Dimes month, but the next day Mama would collect dimes in the neighborhood, and other mothers on her list would walk their areas, too.

"I will also collect dimes," Mrs. Wakamutsu said. "This is a cause for all of us. Next summer could be a worse year for polio. We do not want Miyoko or Laura to get the disease."

Laura had thought the fear of the disease was good for the kids at school, but she didn't like it linked to herself. She remembered those horrible days last summer when first thing every morning she had checked her fingers and toes to make sure they still worked.

"We should make a lot of money for the March of Dimes," Mama explained to Mrs. Wakamutsu. "The whole country is behind the effort. When a movie star like Mary Pickford can take time to be the honorary head of the women's drive, then you know we'll have a successful collection. Last week Jack Benny mentioned the drive on his radio show." She laughed. "If a skinflint like him is going to donate a dime, then everyone should."

"We listened to his funny show in Wyoming," Mrs. Wakamutsu said. "Sachiko sent us a radio after she got her job."

Since Mama didn't need her at the office, and she didn't have homework, Laura asked if she could walk over to Yvonne's.

"Be home before five. Would you like Miyoko to go with you?"

"No," Laura said. "I need to talk to Yvonne alone."

Laura didn't call Yvonne before she walked over. If Yvonne knew she was coming, she might go somewhere. Laura dreaded the confrontation, but she wanted things worked out between them. It was time for Laura to face her fear, as Maude would say. Yvonne had been too good a friend to desert her just because she didn't understand that Miyoko wasn't a real Jap. She just looked like one.

Yvonne's mother opened the door and invited Laura inside. "Yvonne's in her room doing homework," she said. "I'll get her."

Laura walked over to the piano and looked at the display of photographs in various-sized frames. There were Yvonne's parents in their wedding portrait and another photo taken in their wedding attire with their parents on each side, a family portrait of Yvonne with her parents and her brother, Yvonne's grandparents beside a sign that Laura couldn't read since it was in a foreign language, one of Charlie in his navy uniform before that awful day at Pearl Harbor, and several old school pictures of Yvonne and Charlie.

"What are you doing here?" Yvonne asked the moment she came in the room. Her voice was low, probably so her mother wouldn't hear her being rude.

"Just looking at pictures," Laura said. "Aren't these your grandparents?"

"Yeah, so?"

"Where was this picture taken?" Laura had a good idea of the location, but she had to get Yvonne to say for sure.

"When they went to Europe."

"What country were they in? I can't make out the writing on this sign." Laura picked up the photograph. "It looks like German."

Yvonne's glance at Laura was lightning fast, but Laura saw the suspicion in her eyes. "So?"

"Why did they go to Germany?"

"That's where my grandfather was born," Yvonne said, "but he came to this country when he was only three years old. He went back to see what it was like."

"Then you're a Nazi," Laura said.

"I am not! That's the stupidest thing you've ever said, Laura Edwards."

"Is your father in the army?"

"No, but neither is yours."

"Miyoko's father is. Her grandfather was born in Japan but came here when he was a young man. Her father was born in California, and so was she. She's not a Jap. She's as American as you are."

Yvonne was silent for a moment.

"But she looks like a Jap."

"And you look like a German." Laura touched Yvonne's blond hair.

"Why was she sent to the camp if she's not a Jap?"

"I don't know. Maude thinks it was fear because she looked like the enemy, but sending Miyoko's family to the relocation center wasn't called for. It was a mistake," Laura said. "Her mother died there," she added to make Yvonne view Miyoko with more sympathy. "They buried her in Wyoming. Miyoko can't even go put flowers on her grave."

Yvonne frowned and looked thoughtful. "We can't go to Charlie's grave, either, since he's buried on that ship in Pearl Harbor. I need to think about this."

"Me, too," Laura admitted. She wouldn't push Yvonne, because she knew her friend would come to the right conclusion. "You want to ask your mom if you can go with us to the movies on Saturday?"

CHAPTER 9

The Plan Backfires

That evening Laura was quite pleased with herself for convincing Yvonne that Miyoko was an American instead of the enemy. Laura felt sure that Yvonne believed that now, even though she hadn't actually said it. But when Laura went to school the next day, there were two Japanese boys in her own classroom, and most of the class snubbed them. Only Laura and one other boy, Tony Ricci, went out of their way to talk to the boys.

Mrs. Jamison had the Japanese boys draw something for the class banner. Before going outside with the rest of the class for recess, Laura climbed on a chair and pinned on the two new drawings. The only spaces left were right next to the one with the big *X* over the bucktoothed Jap.

On the playground, Laura saw Eddie playing kickball. He'd set his mind on playing that game, and he'd made it happen. He'd taken the other kids' attitudes and turned them around. Instead of ridiculing his impairment, now they admired him for overcoming it.

The two Japanese boys from her classroom stood off to themselves instead of joining in a game with the others. A lone Japanese girl stood by the fence. Thankfully it wasn't Miyoko. Yvonne was actually talking to her over by the swings.

Something had to be done to make others accept the Japanese, but what? The country was at war with the Japs. Laura's classmates had worked hard to raise money to fight the Japs, and now she expected them to welcome yellow-skinned, slant-eyed classmates? She couldn't erase their hatred for Japs as easily as she had convinced Yvonne to talk to Miyoko. Or could she?

Laura walked with purpose back into the school and found Mrs. Jamison at her desk grading arithmetic tests. She explained her idea to her teacher, who looked thoughtful and then said it was worth a try.

As soon as the kids were called in from recess, Mrs. Jamison began the social studies lesson.

"Yesterday we talked about the potato famine forcing a great many Irish to immigrate to the United States. Does anyone have an ancestor who was Irish?" Three or four students held up their hands. "Did any of your grandparents or great-grandparents come to this country in the late 1840s?"

This time there were no hands raised. Finally Eileen O'Brien spoke up. "I don't know when my father's parents came here, but we celebrate St. Patrick's Day every year."

"That's a fun celebration," Mrs. Jamison said. "We all like wearing something green on March 17, even if we don't have a drop of Irish blood."

"My mom has a shamrock plant," Casey Doyle said.

"Good," Mrs. Jamison said. "That's another thing we associate with the Irish. Are any of your families from England?"

Laura and a smattering of other children held up their hands.

"My ancestors came over on the *Mayflower*," Laura said with pride. "They were Pilgrims."

"Can others of you trace your family back to the first colonies?" Mrs. Jamison asked.

No one held up a hand.

"Jeff, do you know when your family came here from England?" Mrs. Jamison asked.

"No, but maybe I could find out."

"That's a great idea. Would each one of you find out who your ancestors were and where they came from and when they came to this country? If your parents don't know, perhaps you can ask your grandparents. We'll each share our stories in social studies tomorrow."

Laura told her idea to Eddie, Miyoko, and Yvonne as they walked home from school. "Tomorrow everyone will tell how many generations they have been in this country. Then they will see that we're all Americans."

"Good. Maybe then Kenny will walk home with us," Eddie said.

"Have you talked to him?" Laura asked.

"No. He won't talk. He just plays with the other boys at recess. Where did he go after school?"

"Sorry, I didn't notice, but I will tomorrow. I'll ask him if he wants to go to the movie with us on Saturday. How's that?"

"Okay," Eddie said and scurried on ahead of the girls.

He was already alone in the office when Laura and Miyoko climbed the stairs to the lobby.

"Mama and Mrs. Wakamutsu are doing the March of Dimes," he said. "Corrine was working here when I came in."

The mailman clomped up the stairs early and handed a bundle of letters to Eddie.

Laura wanted to follow Miyoko to the apartment for a drink, but she went inside the office instead. Sorting the mail kept her in the know about what was going on in the hotel.

"Oh, no," Eddie said. He handed Laura a letter for Mr. Arnold.

Laura read the return address and gasped. "A letter from a dead soldier. Oh, I wonder when Dale wrote this."

She figured that Mama would send it on to Mr. Arnold, whose things had been shipped to Albuquerque the day before. Today his room was to be cleaned, top to bottom, and Corrine and Margie were moving in there that night.

There was no letter from Bruce and, of course, no letter from Neil for Corrine, but Maude had two letters from Jerry.

Once they had put up the other mail, Laura took the letters and dashed down the hall to Maude's apartment. She wanted to tell her how she had convinced Yvonne that Miyoko was a loyal American and all about the social studies project.

Once again Laura waited while Maude read her son's letters.

"Well, he was still on Guam when he wrote these letters. They were written a week apart but were delivered the same day. Hard to figure how the mail system works in a war zone," Maude said and refolded the second letter, just as she had the first. Laura knew she would read them again and again, then put them with the others.

"Yvonne and Miyoko are friends," Laura announced. "Well, maybe not friends like Yvonne and I are, but they're not enemies anymore." She explained how she had managed to get Yvonne to accept Miyoko and also shared her plan for the social studies class. "I told them my ancestors came over on the *Mayflower*," Laura said proudly. "No one else could trace their families that far back."

"Did you also mention your mother's father?"

"I never knew my grandfather. He died before I was born."

"Your mom's told me a bit about him. You must ask her about him before you go to school tomorrow."

"I will. I'll ask Dad about his parents, too."

"Oh, and Laura, don't get too uppity about your family coming over on the *Mayflower*. My family met them on the shore."

"What are you talking about?"

"As Will Rogers said. . . Oh, you wouldn't know him, but he was a famous man from Oklahoma. Anyway, he said that his people met the boat." Maude laughed. "I'm part Indian. My great-grandmother was Cherokee. I'm not sure what tribe lived around Plymouth Rock, but I suspect I'm related somewhere back there. I can trace my ancestors back to the first Americans. So to my family, your old, old family members were recent immigrants."

Laura nodded, and Maude was still chuckling when Laura left her apartment. Odd—Maude didn't look like an Indian. Oh, her hair was dark all right, but she wasn't real tall, and she didn't have red skin.

Laura stayed at the office where Eddie was giving out mail and talked to him about the ancestor assignment, urging him to do the same thing in his room. There were no Japanese in his class right now, but there were bound to be some soon. All the relocation centers were being closed down, little by little.

After supper that night, Laura cornered her dad and asked about his family. With her pencil in hand, she made notes in her social studies notebook.

"Slow down," she said. "Your mother was from New York and your father from Minneapolis. But where did they come from originally, like Mama's family from England?"

"South Africa."

"South Africa!"

"It's part of the British Commonwealth. I'm sure my ancestors at one time came from England, but I don't know when they immigrated to South Africa and then to America. That's on my father's side. On my mother's side, I think there's some Dutch heritage, but that's way back there."

"Thanks. Where's Mama?"

"She just got back from the big march and is in Mr. Arnold's room helping sort out the girls' things. This move will give you girls some much-needed room. I was sent to get a hammer so I can hang a few pictures."

Laura tagged along down the hall to Mr. Arnold's room, now filled with Corrine's and Margie's belongings. Mama was hanging up dresses.

"Can we talk about my homework, Mama?" Laura asked. "I need to find out about our ancestors."

"Fine, dear. What do you want to know?" Her muffled voice came from the built-in closet, another of Dad's improvements to the hotel.

"I know our ancestors came over on the *Mayflower*. Was that on your mother's side or your father's side or both?"

"Mother's side."

"What about your father's side?"

Mama turned around to face Laura. "It's too bad Grandpa Knopf died before you were born. You would have liked him. You have a lot in common."

"Knopf? That doesn't sound like an English name."

"It's not. It's German."

No! Laura thought. *This can't be true.*

"My father came from Germany when he was a boy."

Laura stepped back. What was her mother saying? That Laura's grandfather was a German?

"But Bruce is fighting the Germans," Laura said.

"He's fighting the Nazis," Mama said. "Honey, haven't you heard us talk about the way German-Americans were treated during World War I?" She answered her own question. "No, I guess you were pretty young when Ginny and Gary asked so many questions about it before the war."

"But, Mama, we can't be German," Laura protested.

"You are part German, and it's a heritage to be proud of," Mama said with an edge to her voice. "The Germans are a hardworking people."

Laura looked down at her social studies notebook. She had been so proud that her people had come over on the *Mayflower*. Now she added "German" to the list.

The next day at school, Laura met Yvonne at recess before Miyoko came outside.

"My grandfather was German," Laura blurted out. She'd struggled with the idea of keeping it a secret, but that wouldn't be fair to Yvonne after she had sort of tricked her into accepting Miyoko as an American. Maude always said, "Face your fear," and that was exactly what she was doing.

"What?" Yvonne asked, although Laura was quite sure she'd heard her.

"I thought you should know that my grandpa Knopf came over from Germany, too."

"So we both have ancestors in Germany that we're fighting against," Yvonne said.

"I guess so. I'll bet there are others in my class who didn't know they had German ancestors."

"But they may not tell it," Yvonne said.

"I didn't want to tell you," Laura admitted.

Miyoko joined them, so they dropped the subject and played a game of hopscotch before recess was over.

"Okay, class, it's time for social studies," Mrs. Jamison said when Laura was back in class. "I hope you asked your parents about your ancestors. Who wants to go first? I'll write the different countries on the blackboard."

Keith Rhodes held up his hand. "My dad's family is from England and my mom's is from England, too."

"When did they come to America?" Mrs. Jamison asked.

"A long time ago, but they don't know when," Keith said.

"All right." She wrote ENGLAND on the board. "Johnny?"

"Both my parents are from England, but I don't know when they came here."

This wasn't going according to Laura's plan. Were all the kids going to say they came from England? As much as she didn't want to do it, she held up her hand.

"Laura?"

"Well, I told everyone yesterday that my ancestors came over on the *Mayflower*, and they did. But that was just on my mother's mother's side. On my dad's mother's side, they are Dutch people. On my dad's father's side, they came from South Africa."

There were low *oohs* from some students after Laura mentioned that exotic location. She explained about South Africa belonging to England at one time. Then Laura took a deep breath and said, "My mom's father was from Germany."

"Germany!" Keith spat out the name with disgust.

"He came over when he was a boy," Laura said defensively. "He was a hardworking German, but he wasn't a Nazi!" If she could have, she would have busted Keith right in the nose for making this confession so hard.

"Of course he wasn't," Mrs. Jamison said. She wrote THE NETHERLANDS, SOUTH AFRICA, and GERMANY on the board. Turning back to the class, Mrs. Jamison said, "Tony Ricci, where are your ancestors from?"

"My mama's family is from England, but I don't know when they came over. And my papa's family is from Italy. Papa came over from Italy when he was ten."

"Fascist!" Keith exclaimed.

Tony jumped to his feet with his fists raised.

"That's enough, Keith," Mrs. Jamison said sharply. "Sit down, Tony." She wrote ITALY on the board, then turned around.

"Isamu?"

The new student said in a clear voice, "My parents came to this country seventeen years ago. They were from Japan, but I am an American."

"Dirty Jap," Keith muttered.

This time Laura was on her feet with Tony, and they both went after Keith!

CHAPTER 10

Good-Bye to a President

"Laura Edwards, I'm surprised at you," Mrs. Jamison said. She had taken Laura, Tony, and Keith out into the hall after she gave the students a reading assignment.

"Me? What about the others?" Laura said, although she was a bit surprised at her own reaction to Keith's name-calling. She had never hit anyone in her life, except Eddie, and that had been a long time ago. She hadn't actually hit Keith. Good sense had taken over once Mrs. Jamison had ordered them back to their desks. But Laura had wanted to hit him.

"You want to start World War III?" Mrs. Jamison asked instead of answering the question. "This assignment was to make things better, not worse. Tony, you must hold your temper. You two boys apologize to each other."

Tony looked at Keith and muttered, "I'm sorry," in a sullen manner. Keith did the same.

"Go back into the room, Tony, and get out your reading book."

Tony walked back inside. Mrs. Jamison took Laura and Keith by the arms and walked them farther down the hall, out of earshot of the students in the classroom.

"Now, Keith, I want you to straighten up. What's your problem with Americans who have been here only one or two generations?"

"I don't have a problem," Keith said.

"I think I'll have a talk with your parents," Mrs. Jamison said.

"No," Keith said quickly. "They're real busy working for the war."

"I'll call them tonight," Mrs. Jamison said, "unless you want to tell me what it is that has you calling people names."

"Are you really English on both sides?" Laura asked.

"Yes," Keith said so defensively that Laura suspected that he wasn't. He had straight black hair and a round face, but that didn't tell her anything about his heritage.

"That's not the issue here," Mrs. Jamison said. "Laura, apologize to Keith. You, too," she ordered Keith.

"Sorry," Laura mumbled in a low voice at the same time that Keith muttered something she couldn't make out.

"You may go back in the room," Mrs. Jamison told Laura.

Before she slipped into the room, Laura glanced back and saw Mrs. Jamison wagging a finger at Keith. She hoped he got in deep trouble.

When Mrs. Jamison and Keith came back into the room, the social studies lesson continued. Students gave their information, and the teacher wrote it on the board.

"We have nineteen countries represented," Mrs. Jamison said. "Our textbook calls America a 'melting pot' of nationalities. Wouldn't you agree that that's true?"

The students nodded. Maybe the lesson had an effect on them, but Laura had thought there would be an instant opening of arms to the Japanese boys. There was not. Looking at ancestors had worked for Yvonne, but her family had been in the country the same length of time as Miyoko's, just from a different country.

Laura held up her hand. The class seemed subdued, as if no

one wanted to cause a stir because of the earlier outburst. Maybe she could lighten the moment.

"Yes, Laura?"

"My neighbor Maude," she explained, "says her ancestors met the *Mayflower*."

Mrs. Jamison chuckled, just as Maude had, but the rest of the class didn't. Maybe it was grown-up humor.

"What does she mean by that?" Mrs. Jamison asked the class.

A boy held up his hand, and the teacher nodded at him. "Indians were here first."

"Exactly. Laura's Maude must have some Indian blood." Mrs. Jamison cast a sidelong glance at Keith, and Laura figured that he was part Indian and didn't want to say it. That fit with his straight hair, but his skin wasn't red. And what was wrong with admitting that he was part Indian if he was?

"Who exactly is an American?" Mrs. Jamison said. No one answered. "Would all American citizens please stand up?"

The entire class stood.

"So we're all Americans," she said. "Someday you will all have the right to vote in our democracy. Does your vote count more if your family has lived here longer?"

"No," Tony said before a chorus of other voices answered the same thing.

"Then it's our duty to be good citizens, which includes respecting other people's opinions." At this point she glanced at Laura, who looked down at her desk.

Her grand idea of making the Japanese be accepted hadn't really worked. Her classmates had been hammered with anti-Jap sentiments for too long. It would take more than one social studies lesson to undo that, especially when the war went on and on.

At least the class discussion persuaded Kenny to accept Miyoko—or at least not to object to her when she was in a group with him. He went with Laura, Miyoko, Yvonne, and Eddie that Saturday to see *Meet Me in St. Louis*.

Fighting in the Philippines was on the newsreel. Laura mentioned it to Corrine when they got back to the hotel after the movie, and Corrine burst into tears.

Laura hugged her. "The newsman said we were taking back ground."

"I know, but I'm so afraid they will find graves," Corrine said. "I'm afraid Neil is dead."

Laura had known that all along, so she was surprised that Corrine had just now come to that conclusion. "Maude says we should face our fears." She went through Maude's reasoning about the worst that could happen. "So we pray that God was with him," Laura said.

"*Is* with him," Corrine said with a catch in her voice. "I'll pray that God is with him, that his time on earth isn't over, and that I'll see him again. You're a smart girl, Laura."

"Maude's smart. She's the one who told me to face my fears," Laura admitted, although she raised her chin just a little bit higher.

Soon the news was full of the Russians finding a concentration camp at Auschwitz. Thousands of Jews had been killed, and many were starving to death in the camp.

"What if Neil is in a horrible death camp like that?" Corrine was beside herself again.

"You keep praying that God is with him," Laura said.

"Yes, you're right," Corrine said and fingered the cross on the necklace that Neil had given her before he'd gone into the navy. "I tell Neil's mother that whenever she calls. I just need to remind myself."

The war droned on and on. Letters from Bruce were further apart. He was in Belgium, and Laura figured it was just a matter of time before he'd be in Germany itself. She looked at the atlas whenever a new letter arrived, and she looked at the atlas when she heard a specific town mentioned on the news. Never before had she been aware of the countries of Europe. Now she thought she would never forget them.

She liked the newsreels. There she could see actual moving pictures of the war and of the leaders. In the newspaper, she saw President Roosevelt sitting with England's Churchill and Russia's Stalin when they met at the Yalta Conference, but on the newsreel it looked more real. Laura looked up Yalta in the atlas and had a hard time finding the Crimean port in the Black Sea.

"Why did they pick this place instead of somewhere in the United States?" Laura asked her dad. Yalta was in Asia, but wasn't there always a risk of a German airplane dropping a bomb any-where over there?

"It's hard for us to understand everything about politics," Dad said. "They have more information than we do, and I'm sure President Roosevelt is doing the best he can to end this war."

During March the government asked the public not only to conserve paper, but to turn in all scrap paper to collection centers. A special appeal went to the Boy Scouts. The War Production

Board would award the General Eisenhower Waste Paper Medal to any Boy Scout who collected at least a thousand pounds of waste paper during the March and April campaign.

"Why didn't they ask Girl Scouts?" Laura asked Eddie after he returned from his Scout meeting one afternoon.

He shrugged. "Don't ask me. Since the Girl Scouts aren't doing it, why don't you girls help Kenny and me collect paper?"

"Sure," Laura said, but she'd rather have had a project of her own. In the past, she might have objected to helping Eddie, since they were always in competition. But since he'd had polio, she looked at him differently. In an odd way, the disease had brought them even closer together.

Laura, Yvonne, and Miyoko banded together with Eddie and Kenny to collect every scrap they could. Besides the collection site set up in the lobby where residents could put their old newspapers, the kids went door-to-door, much as they and other students had for the grease drives to get fat for ammunition at the beginning of the war.

They walked up and down the street, asking the businesses there for waste paper. The cigar store had some stuff. Eddie and Kenny went into the labor union office, where men hung around in front. They came back empty-handed but told the girls what the dark, smoke-filled place was like inside.

Not to be outdone, Yvonne marched past the closed ticket booth and knocked on the door of the burlesque house, a place Laura had been forbidden to go near. Mama's exact words were, "Don't go within ten feet of that place." Laura stood by the curb, as far away from the door as she could be and still see the action.

A quite ordinary-looking woman answered the door. Laura

had expected a garish woman in an outlandish costume, but the woman seemed nice, and she brought back old programs and gave them to Yvonne.

"We're supposed to go by every week, and she'll have more," Yvonne said.

"Let's put them at the bottom of the pile," Laura suggested. No need in rousing Mama's curiosity over something that she hadn't done wrong. Laura hadn't gone within ten feet of the place. She'd probably been eleven feet away.

Their pile of papers grew. Eddie and Kenny took them to the collection center and had them weighed and the poundage added to their accounts.

One April day as Laura and the others walked home from school, they talked about going back out after supper and collecting again. They were only a half block from the hotel when they met a young woman with tears streaming down her face.

Without a moment's hesitation, Laura stepped in front of the woman.

"What's wrong? Can we help you?" Laura asked.

The woman, wiping her tears with a handkerchief, looked down at Laura. "The president is dead," she whispered with a sob.

"President Roosevelt?" Eddie said.

"Yes. What will the country do now? Who will lead us through this war?"

"President Roosevelt is dead?" Laura asked. Surely the woman was mistaken. Laura had seen pictures of him at that Yalta Conference. "Did someone kill him?"

"No. The radio said he died of a cerebral hemorrhage."

"A what?" Eddie asked.

"Like a stroke," the woman said and sniffed into her handkerchief.

"Let's go," Laura said. She didn't really believe this woman. She needed to hear it from the radio.

The friends ran to the hotel as fast as they could. The radio was on in the lobby and several residents, including Mr. Benedetto and Mrs. Lind, were sitting around listening to it. Mrs. Wakamutsu sat in the office.

"Is it true? Is President Roosevelt dead?" Laura asked her.

"Yes," she replied.

Laura ran to the apartment, with the other kids on her heels. Mama, Corrine, Ginny, Gary, and the Wakamutsu boys were crammed in the living room, some sitting, some standing. No one was talking except the announcer on the radio. Laura sat on the floor and listened.

While the message from the sponsor was on, Mama said, "He was in Warm Springs, Georgia, at the Little White House. That's the headquarters of the March of Dimes." She wiped away a tear.

"Who is Harry Truman?" Eddie asked.

"The vice president, of course," Ginny said. "Well, president, now."

"What will happen?" Laura asked.

"Nothing different," Corrine said. "I suspect President Truman will continue with President Roosevelt's policies. The war plan will go forward."

"I wonder how Mrs. Roosevelt is bearing up," Mama said.

The newscaster was back on and repeated the news he had already given. The group sat in silence once again, listening.

Laura didn't go out collecting papers. She sat glued to the radio, listening, hoping the announcer would say there had been a bad mistake. She went to bed hoping to wake up the next day and learn this had all been a nightmare. She had liked the president. He'd had polio, like Eddie, which made her feel a special bond with him.

The next morning the nightmare didn't go away. The newspaper headline screamed that President Roosevelt was dead. War news went on for pages. The American army had pushed beyond the Elbe River. At one point, only seventy-five miles separated the Russian and American troops, with Berlin in between. Laura should have looked it up on the map, but she didn't feel like it. Another article said more than four hundred B-29 Superfortresses had bombed Tokyo for two hours. That plane had been designed at the Boeing plant. Laura should have felt proud, but all she felt was numb.

Laura couldn't shake this unsettled feeling. She wondered about the future of the country. How did President Truman feel now that he was the leader of the nation? Like she did sometimes when she was in charge of the class meetings and selling the war stamps?

"Face your fear," she said aloud. She prayed that God had been with President Roosevelt when he died and that He would be with President Truman now.

CHAPTER 11

The Balloon Bomb

Laura read everything she could about the new president. She and the other students in Mrs. Jamison's class listened to Harry Truman's speech to Congress the day after President Roosevelt had been laid to rest in New York.

"He's asked the country to help him and asked for God's help," Maude told Laura after school. "Can't ask for more than that. Besides, he's from Missouri, right next door to Oklahoma. That means he's got common sense."

Later, on the newsreel at the movie, Laura, Miyoko, and Yvonne saw Harry Truman being sworn in as president. The newsreel was also full of pictures from the death camps in Germany. The pictures of half-starved people in Buchenwald and Belsen made Laura sick.

Yvonne leaned over Laura and whispered to Miyoko, "It wasn't like that where you were, was it?"

"Oh, no. We were in small quarters and the food was not very good, but it was nothing like that."

"I'm glad German descendants weren't sent to relocation centers or internment camps," Yvonne said.

Laura was, too.

"My relatives didn't do this to those people," Yvonne said and motioned to the screen where pictures of the concentration camps still flickered.

"Or mine," Laura said.

"And mine didn't bomb Pearl Harbor," Miyoko said.

What a mixed-up time, Laura thought. *Countries do horrible things to each other, yet ordinary people wouldn't do such bad things.*

Mrs. Jamison had the students bring in newspaper clippings about the United Nations Conference that started at the end of April in San Francisco. The class talked about how many nations would likely join and how this would be a way to keep the world at peace.

"The United Nations might be a 'melting pot,' just like the United States," Mrs. Jamison said, and Laura hoped that would be true.

Troops were closing in on Berlin, but the war effort on the home front continued as the paper drive came to a close.

Eddie and Kenny and the girls carried a load of scrap paper to the collection center on Saturday after they finished morning chores. They'd been carrying paper forever, it seemed. And every time they went to the center, Eddie's and Kenny's accounts went up fifteen or twenty pounds.

"What does this make it?" Eddie asked after the paper was weighed in.

"Almost there. Just another twenty-two pounds," the collection worker said.

Kenny's load was weighed in and came to twenty-four pounds. He still needed eighteen more.

"Monday's the end of the month, boys. This place will be a

madhouse then. If you can, bring more paper this afternoon."

"We've already been to all our collection sites. Where else can we go?" Laura asked as they made their way to the hotel.

"We haven't been back to the burlesque house," Yvonne said. She'd told her mom about that collection place and had been forbidden to return. "That woman probably has tons of old programs for us."

"But we can't go there again," Eddie said. "None of us is allowed to go near that place."

"I have an idea," Laura said. "Maybe under the circumstances, my mother and Mrs. Wakamutsu would give us one-time permission to go there, just to get the paper. It is for the war, after all."

"What do we have to lose?" Kenny asked, and the group raced off to the hotel.

To their relief, both Mama and Mrs. Wakamutsu were home. As soon as Eddie explained the problem, the two women looked at each other. Laura held her breath.

"Because this is for the war," Mama said slowly, "you may go this one time."

Laura started breathing again.

"But," Mama continued, "it is not a good place for you to be, and you are not to go near there again. Is that understood?"

Laura and Eddie nodded.

"Miyoko," Mrs. Wakamutsu said, "you may also go. It will be a way to help your father win the war. But be careful."

The five friends walked briskly toward the hotel, but when they approached the burlesque house, they slowed their pace and looked nervously at each other.

"Who's going to knock on the door?" Kenny asked. No one answered him.

"I will go ask," Miyoko finally said. She walked to the door and knocked softly.

A man answered. "What do you want, little Jap?" he barked.

Miyoko stepped back.

"Scrap paper collection for the Boy Scouts."

"You don't look like no Boy Scout." He looked at Laura and the others. "You with them?"

"I am collecting for my father, who is a soldier."

"I'll bet. For the emperor!" he said and slammed the door.

Laura marched to the door and pounded on it.

"Hey, mister!" she called.

The man opened the door. "I thought—what's this?"

"My friend's dad is in the United States Army in Europe. Now do you have any scrap paper for the drive? Any old programs?"

"What is it?" a voice called from behind the man. The woman Laura had seen before came to the door. This time she wore heavy makeup and a glittery dress. She looked at the kids, and Laura saw recognition in her eyes when she spotted Yvonne. "Oh, I wondered when you'd come back for the papers. They've been piling up. Hurry up, kids. In a few minutes we'll be opening the ticket booth for the afternoon show. I want you out of here before then."

Laura led the way and motioned for the others to follow. She strained to look around, but they were led down a closed hallway, so she couldn't even see the stage.

There had to be a ton of paper in the huge pile in the back room. The five friends loaded up until they could carry no more and trudged to the front door. Before they left, Laura turned to the woman. "Miyoko's father is fighting in the 442nd. He's a war hero. Tell that man."

"I'll tell him, honey, but I doubt it'll do much good."

"Thank you for the papers," Eddie said as they filed out of the burlesque house and headed to the collection center.

Laura walked alongside Miyoko. "Sorry about that man."

"It is not your fault," Miyoko said and shrugged. "I am used to it."

The kids struggled along under their loads in silence, an oddity for them.

"We're back," Eddie said fifteen minutes later when they dumped their loads on the scales.

The man looked at the programs, then said, "I guess paper's paper no matter where you got it."

Between the five of them, they had fifty-seven pounds. The man divided the number between Kenny's and Eddie's accounts and proclaimed them both winners of the Eisenhower medal.

"Wow!" Eddie exclaimed. "When do we get it?"

"Your troop leader will award it," the man said.

The kids walked with light steps back toward the hotel. As they neared the burlesque house again, Kenny said, "It took guts to knock on that door, Miyoko. You earned part of the medal."

"I will take a corner piece," she said.

"What?" Kenny said.

Miyoko giggled, the first time Laura had ever heard her laugh. "It is a joke," she said.

"I'll let you wear it sometime," Kenny said, and Laura vowed silently to hold him to that promise.

During the following week, tension mounted in the hotel as news from the European front gave hope that the end of the war was likely to occur at any moment. With the news of Hitler's suicide, Laura rejoiced. Surely that meant that the war couldn't go on any longer. But the Germans held out for another week. Finally the official announcement came from President Truman. The Germans had unconditionally surrendered.

Laura's first reaction was that Bruce would be coming home, safe and sound. Miyoko's father would come home, too.

But President Truman's V-E Day broadcast that she heard before she went to school and again in Mrs. Jamison's room made Laura rethink the situation.

"Our victory is but half-won," the president said. "The West is free, but the East is still in bondage to the treacherous tyranny of the Japanese. When the last Japanese division has surrendered unconditionally, only then will our fighting job be done."

Mrs. Jamison made the issue crystal clear when she followed the announcement of the victory in Europe with a secret warning to the students.

"I'm going to tell you a story, and I want you to take it to heart. It's very important that you know this, but in a way it's a secret," she began.

"Last Saturday the Reverend Archie Mitchell, his wife Elsie, and four boys and a girl from their church went on a picnic in the south part of Oregon. It's unclear exactly what happened. Reverend Mitchell was parking the car when his wife called out for him to come see what they had found. There was a loud explosion, and Reverend Mitchell found the five children dead and his wife barely alive and her clothes on fire. He burned his hands trying to put out the flames, but his wife died within minutes. The children had found a Japanese balloon that held bombs."

Gasps echoed around the room, and Laura looked at the wide-eyed stares of the other students.

"I suspect that someone touched the balloon or one of the bombs itself, and it exploded," Mrs. Jamison said. "It made a hole three feet across, and there was shrapnel everywhere. If any of you see such a balloon, you are to run away from it and report it immediately to the police."

"How many are there?" Laura asked.

"I don't know."

"Where are they coming from?" Keith asked.

"The authorities are unsure. It could be that a Japanese ship has released them, or it could be that they have been released from the island of Japan itself. Perhaps there are no more of them, but the government doesn't want the Japanese to know that any balloons have landed here.

"That's where the secret comes in. The government wants no mention of this on the radio or in the newspapers. If the Japanese find out they have been successful, they may send more balloon bombs. But be sure to tell your parents and your brothers and sisters and others that you trust. They should be warned."

"What do the balloons look like?" a student asked.

"I haven't seen one, but the principal told us they were made of rubberized silk or layers of paper and string. The balloon part is thirty feet across, and the bombs hang below it. They can be pearl gray in color. Don't touch them! Remember, there will be no reports of this in the newspapers or on the radio. We don't want the Japanese to know the balloons are reaching us.

"What's the motto? 'Loose lips. . . ,'" Mrs. Jamison started.

" 'Sink ships,' " the class said in unison.

"Three of the children killed were thirteen. One boy was fourteen, and one was eleven. Be careful and be watchful, boys and girls. I don't want to lose any of you. Now, you can go out for recess a little early."

The students filed silently out of the room and headed for the playground. There was no laughing and poking each other, like the boys normally did when they went outside.

As soon as the other classes had recess, Laura and Kenny found the others. "Did your teacher tell you about the balloon bomb?" she asked.

"Yeah. . .one boy was my age," Eddie said quietly.

That night Laura told both families about the balloons.

"President Truman is right," Dad said. "We have reason to celebrate tonight, but the war is only half-won. I wonder if Bruce will be sent to the Pacific."

Laura hadn't thought of that possibility. Now she murmured, "God be with him."

CHAPTER 12

Good-Bye, Hotel

"I'm worried about Jerry," Maude confessed to Laura one afternoon while she was working in the office alone. Eddie and Kenny were at Boy Scouts, and Mama and Mrs. Wakamutsu were cleaning out another empty room for some repair work.

"Why?"

"It's been over a month since I heard from him. I'm afraid he's been sent to Okinawa."

Laura got out the atlas, and they looked at the distance from Guam to the bigger island. The United States had already taken Iwo Jima from the Japanese, and the newsreel showed it had taken heavy fighting to win. Japanese soldiers hid artillery guns in caves and rained bullets on Americans. Radio reports from the Pacific talked about hand-to-hand combat.

"There isn't an American airfield on Okinawa yet, is there?" Laura asked. Since they'd learned from the code that Jerry worked at keeping planes flying, it made sense that he would be at an airfield. "Maybe he's been sent to Iwo Jima."

"Maybe."

"Face your fear," Laura reminded her.

"I know, but the Japanese fight until they're killed. And I don't know what to think of the kamikaze pilots. Those men know they're going to die before they climb in their airplanes."

"They must be crazy," Laura said. She'd seen a picture in the newspaper of a wrecked kamikaze plane burning on the deck of an American ship. She and Yvonne had talked about how insane those Japanese were to ram their planes into ships in the hopes of sinking them. They had been careful not to talk about it in front of Miyoko. Her entire heritage was from Japan, and she observed some of their customs. Laura didn't feel comfortable talking about the Pacific war in front of her.

"You know what I think, Laura?" Maude said in a low voice. "I've started looking at each one of these men as someone's son. For every one killed, there's a mother out there who will never be the same."

"But we're at war," Laura said. "It's our country against their country. If we don't kill them, they'll kill us."

"I know, but that doesn't make it right," Maude said.

"Mail here?" Mrs. Lind called from a little way down the hall.

"Yes, ma'am," Laura said. "You have a letter."

Mrs. Lind didn't get a lot of mail, and what she got was usually postmarked from Atlanta. Laura handed over the letter and the afternoon newspaper. Then she turned her attention back to the map.

"American troops are getting closer and closer to Japan," Maude said. "It's just a matter of time before they invade, but if the little islands have caused such fierce fighting, I can't imagine what the soldiers will face on Japan."

"*Nooo!*"

Laura looked at the couch when she heard the groan of anguish. The letter fluttered to Mrs. Lind's lap. Tears streamed down her face.

"Mrs. Lind!" Maude reached her first. "What is it?"

Mrs. Lind motioned to the letter, and Maude picked it up and quickly scanned it.

"Is this your sister's boy?"

Mrs. Lind nodded.

"Laura, get your mother."

With wings on her feet, Laura ran to the room where Mama and Mrs. Wakamutsu were working. "Hurry, it's Mrs. Lind," Laura said and fled back to the lobby. Laura felt helpless, just as she had when Mr. Arnold's Dale had been killed. The end of the war seemed near with victory in sight, but still men were dying.

Mama, Mrs. Wakamutsu, and Maude took Mrs. Lind back to her apartment. Mrs. Wakamutsu came to the office and told Laura that Mrs. Lind's nephew was missing in action on Okinawa. To Laura that meant he was dead, just like she knew Neil Palmer was dead.

Supper was a quiet affair with the news of Mrs. Lind's nephew hanging over the two families. Mama had helped her call her sister from the office and later had taken a tray of food to her apartment.

"Will she go to her sister's?" Eddie asked.

"No. She'll stay here and wait for news," Mama said.

"She could have a long wait," Corrine said quietly.

Laura looked at her sister, who had tears welling in her eyes. When would it all be over? When would they know the truth about Neil? Someone at school had told her it was seven years after a war before a missing-in-action person could be declared dead. Corrine was twenty-four now. In seven years she'd be thirty-one, an old maid. Laura doubted she would go out with any man on a date during that seven years. She sure hadn't gone out since Neil had been sent to the Philippines.

Dad called a family meeting in the living room after supper dishes were done.

He started with a prayer for Mrs. Lind and her nephew and, of course, remembered Bruce, Neil, Jerry, Leonard Ito, and all the soldiers fighting the war.

After prayer, Dad cleared his throat. "Your mother and I have decided something," he said slowly. "Although the war isn't over yet, I think it will be soon. When that happens, not as many jobs will be needed at Boeing—especially for the women—and when Bruce comes home, we'll need even more room as a family. Money isn't as tight as it has been, and I'd like for us to have a fresh start." He paused. "We've decided to sell the hotel and move to a house in Laurelhurst, away from the city," Dad finished.

"We're moving?" Eddie asked.

Mama nodded and continued, "We've found a buyer for the hotel, and he has offered Mr. and Mrs. Wakamutsu the job of running it. Now, with school letting out next week, you kids will have time to help me pack our belongings. The new house is just right for us—with lots of room and places to play. . . . There's even a garden in the back. And the house is still close by for a day trip back here."

"I've already arranged for a truck to move our things. Moving day will be on Saturday, June 2," Dad added.

"It'll be different living in a house again," Laura said. There had been many times that she'd wanted to go back to a time before the war, but now she could hardly remember a time when she didn't live at the hotel. She struggled with memories of the house they had lived in before Dad and Mama had purchased the hotel. They certainly had had more room than the current arrangement with the Wakamutsus. And there had been homemade ice cream and cookies. There had been no sugar rationing before the war, so she had taken desserts for granted.

With the move, Laura would be out of a job. Her time in the office would be over. She had come to love that job. Sitting at the hotel desk had made her feel important. What would they do during the summer in their own house? There would be no hallways to scrub and no linens to change. No bustle of people on the street below. No Maude to talk to. No Yvonne. No Miyoko. No Mrs. Lind. A move would mean changing schools again and giving up her position as president of her classroom, the only girl president in the entire school.

She could hardly stand it until the meeting was over. As soon as Dad had finished answering questions, she scurried out the door and down to Maude's apartment.

"What's wrong?" Maude said the minute she opened her door.

"We're moving!" Laura wailed and rushed inside.

"Yes, your mother told me. I'm glad you could finish the school year here, but it'll be nice for your folks to be back in a home of their own."

"But when will I see you?" Laura asked, following Maude to the tiny kitchen. "And what about Yvonne?"

"I can't answer about Yvonne, but you'll see me." Maude got out two glasses and the ice trays. "I have Jerry's car, you know, and I can drive anywhere I want. Electric buses will likely run near your house, and they could drop you off at the corner here, so you could come for the day for next to nothing."

She poured iced tea and handed a glass to Laura, who took a

big gulp. It was unsweetened, of course. After the war, Laura could go back to drinking sweetened tea. There had to be good things about this if they would be able to have sugar again.

"Things will be different," Maude said, "but change is usually good. Look at how you've changed since you moved here."

"How?" Laura asked. She hadn't noticed change. She'd always been the same Laura.

"You and Eddie have become friends instead of being so competitive. And you've been very responsible in the office. You should work for the post office when you get older."

"I want to be a politician," Laura said and was surprised that she'd said that. She hadn't given her future any real thought, but she liked being in charge of things.

Maude nodded. "I believe there will be a time when women will be candidates for the House of Representatives and the Senate. Why, look how Frances Perkins was on President Roosevelt's cabinet all these years. It's just a matter of time until women will be elected."

"Maybe there'll be a woman governor," Laura said.

"Could be. Anything's possible. But you didn't have any idea of running for classroom president before you moved here. See how you've changed? And you'll keep changing."

"Until I'm grown up."

"No, you'll keep changing even after that."

Laura finished her tea and walked down the hall, her head spinning with thoughts of the future. Eddie intercepted her in the lobby.

"What do you think about moving?" he asked.

"It'll be a big change and there'll be a lot of things I'll miss, but there's bound to be some good things, too."

"Like what?" he asked and fell in step with her as they headed to the apartment.

"We'll probably have a big backyard, and maybe Dad or Gary could build us a tree house."

"You're right. I might try to talk Mama into letting me have a dog. I wonder if Kenny. . ." His voice trailed off.

"Maude thinks electric buses run from here to there," Laura said. "Kenny can ride out and play with your dog."

"And we could come downtown some days."

"Sure. See, there are good things," Laura said as she opened the door to the apartment.

The next day at school she repeated that same phrase as she told Yvonne about the move. She'd given it a lot of thought and had several *options*, she called them, a word she'd seen politicians use in the paper.

During the summer, they could form a friendship club. On Tuesdays Yvonne and Miyoko could ride out to Laurelhurst, and on Fridays Laura could come downtown. Or on Mondays she could come to town, and on Thursdays they could come to her house.

"Or we could meet halfway and have lunch," Yvonne said with a high-society accent, when she heard Laura's plan.

Laura laughed. This might work. She'd just have to make the most of it. Probably as the new girl in school next year, she wouldn't be elected classroom president, but she wouldn't worry about that. Right now she had the last-day-of-school picnic to plan and money to collect for the gift the class would give to Mrs. Jamison.

The picnic went off well, with races, tug-of-war, and other games. It was almost time for the class to go inside to get their report cards. That was when they'd give the teacher her gift. Laura was standing by the outside door when Keith walked by.

"Keith, can I talk to you a minute?" He stopped and eyed her suspiciously. "Are you part Indian?" she asked. Laura figured she'd never see him again after this day anyway, but she had wondered since that time she'd almost hit him for making bad comments about other people's ancestors.

He stared at her with dark eyes for a long moment, and she didn't think he would answer her question. "I'm part Eskimo," he finally said. "So what?"

Laura shrugged. "I think that's neat. Why'd you hide it?"

Now he shrugged. "I don't know. But I'm part English, too."

"We're both Americans," Laura said. "It doesn't matter where we came from."

"Maybe," he said.

"Do you want to present the gift to Mrs. Jamison?" she asked impulsively as a gesture of peace.

"Okay. Sure, I'll do it."

Laura called the last class meeting to order when everyone was in from the playground. She gave a report on how many war stamps they had bought during the year, the highest amount in the school. Then she called Keith to the front to make the teacher presentation.

Mrs. Jamison looked stunned as she opened a card that all the students had signed and the gift—some hard-to-get perfume. "This is heavenly," she said. "Such a nice fragrance. Thank you all so much. This is a class I will never forget."

One by one, Mrs. Jamison called her students to the front to receive their report cards. Then the final bell of the year rang, and the class was dismissed. Everyone rushed to the door with shouts of joy about summer vacation.

"Laura Edwards, could I see you for a moment?" Mrs. Jamison asked before Laura could leave.

"Yes, ma'am." Laura couldn't imagine what her teacher wanted. She didn't think she had done anything wrong at the meeting.

The teacher waited until the other students had left; then she turned to Laura. "It's been a real pleasure having you as the class-room president. You're a smart girl. I've known that all along, but today you showed one more sign of it. You read people very well. You can see when they're hurt and when they need help. Now tell me, why did you let Keith give me the card and perfume?"

"I don't know. I guess it was my way of saying I was sorry for the way I almost attacked him that one day. I'll never see him again, since we're moving next weekend, but I didn't want to leave it bad between us."

Mrs. Jamison hugged her. "You're going to go very far in life. Make all good choices, Laura."

"Think I can be governor someday?" Laura asked with a grin.

"I don't know why not. Be sure and invite your old teacher to your inauguration."

The others were waiting to walk home, but Laura couldn't share her teacher's good-bye with them. It was personal and would sound like bragging. There was a time when that wouldn't have stopped her, but Maude was right. She had changed.

CHAPTER 13

The End of the War

The week between school being out and the family's move to Laurelhurst was filled to the brim with work, packing, and saying good-bye.

Maude had a good-bye party for them in the lobby on Friday night. It reminded Laura of the Christmas Eve party when Mr. Arnold had been there.

Since Miyoko had grown attached to Shadow, and it had been the Wakamutsus' cat originally, Margie gave it to Miyoko at the party.

"Shadow's home is at the hotel," Margie said. "It wouldn't be right to make her leave."

"You are very kind," Miyoko said. She held the cat close to her heart.

Minoru presented a pen-and-ink drawing of the hotel to the Edwardses. "So you will remember your time here," he said.

Laura knew that she would never forget it.

On Saturday, Mr. Wakamutsu drove to the front of the hotel in the borrowed truck. Gary, Minoru, and Kiyoshi carried the furniture the family had brought with them down the stairs. Kenny and Yvonne came over to carry boxes, and Ginny, Corrine, Laura, Miyoko, Mrs. Wakamutsu, Mama, and Maude struggled with household goods and boxes of clothes.

Sitting in the office chair was none other than Mrs. Lind. Laura had suggested to Mrs. Wakamutsu that Mrs. Lind could watch the office while the others helped with the move. Laura had remembered how Mrs. Lind had liked it when she'd done that one other time, and right now Mrs. Lind needed something to take her mind off her nephew's missing-in-action status.

Laura was feeling pretty smug. If there was one thing she had learned recently, it was that turning old enemies into friends was a way of helping herself feel good. Not that Mrs. Lind or Keith Rhodes were enemies, but there had been friction between Laura and them in the past. Now that was eased.

Mama, the older girls, and Maude had spent all day Friday at the house getting it cleaned and ready. As soon as everything was loaded, everyone piled into the truck or Maude's car to drive to the house. More of the family's belongings, including chests of drawers and beds, had been stored elsewhere when they had first moved to the hotel. Once those things were loaded onto the truck and brought to the new house, too, the boys wrestled them into the rooms Mama pointed out.

Laura thought her bed-making and sweeping was over with the move from the hotel, but she and Yvonne were put on that detail before they knew it.

"First thing is to make the beds," Mama said. "Then when we're too tired to unpack one more box, we can fall into bed."

Laura and Yvonne went from room to room, carrying clean linens.

"This is a great house," Yvonne said once they were in Laura's room.

"I know. I especially like my room. You can look down at the backyard from the window. Eddie wants to build a tree house in that tree there."

The place buzzed with activity. Maude and Mama worked in the kitchen. Mrs. Wakamutsu helped the girls hang clothes in the built-in closets, and the boys toted box after box from the truck.

"Dad and Margie will be shocked when they see this," Laura said. The living room looked homey with the old familiar couch and chairs facing the fireplace.

At noon, the Wakamutsus departed to return the truck and get back to their work at the hotel. Maude took Mama to the grocery store, and after the food was unloaded, she left, giving Yvonne and Kenny a ride home.

"Well, kids, it's just us," Mama said, looking around her with obvious pleasure. "Seems quiet, doesn't it?"

It almost seemed lonely to Laura, but she still had lots to do, so she worked in her room, getting her things arranged. The smell of baking chocolate drew her to the kitchen.

"What is that?" she asked.

"Chocolate cake. Maude's been saving the chocolate, and I spent my ration on sugar for our first night here." Mama said it with such pleasure that Laura realized the years they had spent at the hotel had been a real sacrifice.

Although there were no pictures on the walls or knickknacks out on the small lamp tables in the living room, the house looked like a home by the time Dad and Margie came to the house from work. Dinner was a festive occasion, and the chocolate cake was cause in itself for celebration.

That night as she lay in bed in the strange room decorated with familiar things, Laura wondered what was going on at the hotel.

On Sunday after Dad and Margie had gone off to work, Laura and the others rode the electric bus downtown to church and then returned to the house. Never had a Sunday afternoon dragged out so long. Sunday afternoons had been family times before the war, but now they weren't a whole family. Dad and Margie were working, and Bruce was gone.

By late Monday morning, everything was in its place in the house, and Laura was at a loss for what to do. Eddie had worked on Gary's old bicycle, but it needed a new tire, and there weren't any available. Ginny's bike was in just as bad shape. When the war was over, he could fix them both up, and maybe he and Laura could ride around in the neighborhood.

Mama called on the neighbors, and Laura and Eddie walked around the area, becoming familiar with places. Eddie's limp seemed more pronounced. Laura wondered if his weakened leg bothered him more in the summer than in the winter, but she didn't ask. She didn't want him to know that she'd noticed.

They talked about the different people they saw in the neighborhood as they passed house after house, and soon their steps led them to a school. The playground was bigger than the one at the school downtown.

Laura's stomach churned a little at the thought of meeting all of the new kids, but she tried to remember how good it felt to befriend Mrs. Lind and Keith Rhodes and determined to be her friendliest when school started in the fall. Maybe she wouldn't be elected classroom president, but she might be vice president. That hope made her step a little lighter.

They walked home and found only Gary and Ginny there.

"Maude called, and Mama and Corrine took the bus downtown. Mrs. Lind was notified that her nephew was killed in action," Ginny said.

"Does that mean they found his body?" Eddie asked.

"I guess it does. Mama said they might not have been able to identify it before," Gary said.

Laura wanted to go to the hotel, but she obeyed Mama's orders to stay home and help with the yard work. After all, she was going downtown tomorrow to meet Yvonne and Miyoko for their first friendship club meeting. Eddie was going, too, since Mama thought the two ought to ride the bus together.

Gary pushed the mower, and Laura and Eddie picked up fallen sticks and pulled weeds out of what had been a Victory garden with tomato plants and onion sets planted by the previous owners.

"I know this garden doesn't look very healthy, but the plants are still little," Laura said. "By the end of summer we could have juicy tomatoes."

They finished the work and waited on the small porch for Mama to return. When she came home, she reported that Mrs. Lind was doing as well as could be expected.

The next afternoon, Laura picked a small bouquet of roses from the climbing bush in the backyard and took them to Mrs. Lind after she and Eddie rode the bus downtown. The girls traded news about what they'd been doing, and Laura was a little annoyed that Yvonne was continuing last summer's habit of visiting the hotel each afternoon. She felt left out but tried to push down that feeling.

Laura visited with Maude a few minutes before the time came for her to meet Eddie at the bus stop and go back home. She also picked up a letter from Bruce that had been delivered to the hotel.

The summer fell into a pattern. Yvonne and Miyoko came out to Laurelhurst on Friday afternoons, and Laura introduced them to some new friends in the neighborhood. Bruce's letters started coming to the house, and although the war news continued to dominate the newspaper, Laura didn't keep up with it as she had when they'd lived in the hotel.

She seemed more removed from it now that school was out and they lived in a house again. There still wasn't much sugar, Mama continued to ride the bus down to the ration board, and Corrine and Ginny continued their volunteer work with the Red Cross, but Laura knew it was just a matter of time now until the war with Japan would be over.

She read of President Truman going to the Potsdam Conference at the end of July and saw his picture in the paper with the Russian and English leaders. Out of habit, she got the atlas off of the bookshelf and found Potsdam right outside of Berlin.

Then the unimaginable occurred. Shortly after eight o'clock one August morning, Dad called home from the Boeing plant. He rarely called, so Laura knew something important had happened. Mama turned white and motioned for Eddie to turn on the radio. The newscaster was repeating a special war bulletin from the president.

"Sixteen hours ago, an American airplane dropped one bomb on Hiroshima. . . . It is an atomic bomb. It is a harnessing of the basic power of the universe. . . ."

"What does that mean?" Ginny asked.

Laura had no idea. She listened to a vague explanation by the newscaster about destroying Japanese docks, factories, and their power to make war.

"It is a most terrible bomb." Mama wrung her hands as she talked. "Dad said it destroyed the entire city."

"Could that happen here?" Laura asked. She had no idea how many balloon bombs had been sent or if any more had landed since her teacher had talked about them to the class. No one talked about them.

"I don't think Japan has the atomic bomb, but this is the place they would drop it if they did. They'd want to destroy the Boeing plant. Dad said it was one of Boeing's B-29s that dropped the bomb."

"Does that mean the end of the war?" Gary asked. "If it destroyed Japan's factories, they can't make airplanes."

"I don't know," Mama said. "I imagine the end of the war is closer. Maybe Bruce will be coming home soon." She reached for the telephone and called the hotel.

Laura heard her talking to Mrs. Wakamutsu.

"What did she say?" Laura asked once Mama had hung up the receiver.

"She's all right about it. Her sister lives in Tokyo, and Miyoko's relatives live in Nagasaki."

Laura breathed a sigh of relief. At least her friends were not directly affected by the bombing.

But a few days later, the newspaper headline screamed about another bombing. This time Nagasaki was hit. Laura and Eddie took the bus to the hotel even though it was Thursday and the girls would be coming to their house the next day.

"How are you?" Laura asked Miyoko.

"I am okay," she said, but she had tears in her eyes. "I don't know if my relatives were killed or injured. I never met them, but my father did. He is still in Germany. I received a letter from him yesterday. I know he must be grieving for his family."

"The Japanese have to surrender now," Eddie said, "or we'll keep bombing their cities. They have to give up. Then your father will come home."

The papers were full of the peace talks. American soldiers stopped bombing while the Allies considered Japan's surrender terms. At the same time, Russian troops invaded Manchuria in Asia, and news reached Seattle about the sinking of the *Indianapolis*, which was torpedoed by a Japanese submarine at the end of July. The ship had sunk in minutes, leaving many sailors adrift in the shark-infested waters for days before rescue ships had arrived. Many sailors had been eaten alive by the sharks.

Laura could hardly imagine such horror. With peace so close, men were still losing their lives in such hideous ways.

Days passed, and Laura and the others hardly dared to breathe, waiting on tenterhooks.

On Tuesday afternoon, Yvonne, Kenny, and Miyoko were walking Laura and Eddie to the bus stop when a yell like Laura had never heard before came out of the labor union office. Men rushed out of the building.

"It's over!" One man's voice could be heard above the cheers.

"Japan surrendered!" another yelled.

Laura screamed. Tears of joy flooded her eyes.

The kids ran back up the sidewalk to the hotel and found people pouring on to the street from every building and business. Church bells rang. Factory whistles shrilled an end to the war. Firecrackers exploded in the alley. Women cried, and old men whooped. Children shouted and danced around on the sidewalk, twirling until they were so dizzy they fell down. The place was in chaos, and it didn't let up. It just got wilder.

Laura tried to call home from the office phone, but she couldn't get through. The lines were jammed.

"Stay here," Maude said. "Your folks will know where you are."

Laura couldn't stay in the hotel when there was such excitement outside and the crowd was growing bigger and bigger. She rushed down the stairs and out on the sidewalk with the others.

From above, it rained feathers like confetti. Laura looked up in time to see Mrs. Lind shaking a pillow's contents on the joyous crowd below.

"It's over!" Laura shouted. "It's over!"

CHAPTER 14

The Homecoming

Mama, Corrine, Gary, and Ginny arrived at the hotel on the bus.

"What a wild ride!" Gary told Laura and the others. "Everyone was crying and shouting and carrying on. It was great!"

Dad and Margie went home after their work shifts, read the note Mama had left, and wound up at the hotel, too. What a party! What a celebration!

"Jerry is coming home!" Maude shouted, hugging everyone in sight. "My son made it through the war."

"Mine, too," Mama said. "I don't think he ever got moved to the Pacific. But we'll find out soon."

Mrs. Wakamutsu smiled but was rather quiet compared to the others. Laura cornered Miyoko and asked her about her foster mother.

"She told me," Miyoko said, "that there is a line that cuts her in two. She loves America. It is now her home. It has been so good to her, and her children are American. Yet her people are in Japan. She feels sorrow for her homeland, but she has no wish to ever return there."

"What about Mr. Wakamutsu?" Laura didn't know him nearly as well as she knew his wife.

"Long ago in the camp, he told me that he felt like a child

whose parents were arguing. He didn't care who won as long as the fighting stopped."

"Well, I'm glad it's over," Laura said.

"Me, too," Miyoko said. "I am a loyal American. I want you to know that is true."

"I know that," Laura said.

Laura's family left the hotel after midnight. The next morning, although Dad and Margie went to work as usual, the rest of the household dragged around, tired but happy.

"When will Bruce get to come home?" Laura asked.

"I don't know," Mama said. "Dad says the army takes awhile to discharge soldiers, and some will be kept overseas to enforce the peace. We've waited this long; I suppose we can wait as long as it takes, now that we know he's coming home."

Exactly a week later, the phone rang. Laura picked it up, expecting Yvonne to be on the other line, but instead a woman's choked-up voice asked for Corrine.

Laura covered the receiver with her hand. "Mama, it's for Corrine," she whispered. "It sounds like a woman crying. I think it's Mrs. Palmer." This was the call that Laura had dreaded for so long.

"Oh, no," Mama said. "I'll get her."

A moment later Corrine walked into the living room with Mama on her heels. Corrine took the phone and said timidly, "Hello?"

She listened for a second, then sank slowly to the floor. She said something that Laura couldn't make out because of her sobs. Tears poured down her cheeks, and her breath came in giant gasps. Finally Laura could understand. "Thank You, God. Thank You, God," Corrine said over and over.

"Is he alive?" Mama asked.

Corrine nodded, and still more tears came. Laura plopped on the floor and hugged her sister.

Mama took the phone. "Mrs. Palmer? Mrs. Palmer? Neil's all right?" She looked at Laura and nodded her head up and down.

Laura wiped her own tears. "Where is he?" she asked, but Corrine could only shake her head.

"Eddie!" Laura yelled toward the stairs. "Eddie!"

He ran down the stairs. After one look at Corrine's face, his mouth flew open, and he turned and yelled, "Gary!"

"Neil's alive," Laura said and found she was having difficulty speaking, too. Both boys came into the living room and hugged Corrine.

Mama hung up the phone and joined the group on the floor. "He was in a prison camp in Manchuria. He's in a hospital in China now."

"Hos. . .pi. . .tal?" Corrine had the hiccups now.

"He's very weak. Prisoners weren't fed very well, but he's going to be all right," Mama said. "He'll be flown to a stateside hospital."

"Thank. . .God," Corrine said.

"Yes, let's thank God right now," Mama said and led her children in prayer.

Ginny came home from a friend's house, and the tears of joy started again as the story was retold. Mama called Dad and the hotel, and Laura called her friends, and the news spread.

Laura still couldn't believe it. As more details were known, she was amazed that Neil had survived. A few days later, he cabled his parents and Corrine and wrote that he'd made it through the Bataan Death March and then was taken to Manchuria from the Philippines, but now he was all right and would be coming home soon.

The days dragged by as August turned into September and the family waited. A triumphant letter arrived from Bruce. When the news of the atomic bombs had reached his unit in Germany, the troops had celebrated. Their orders for the Pacific were canceled, and Bruce knew he'd be coming home soon.

School started, which helped the waiting to go faster. Laura and Eddie were put in the same classroom, which dismayed Laura. Wouldn't Eddie want to run for classroom president or vice president just as she wanted to? And could she run against him?

She didn't have to decide. This school didn't have classroom presidents. Disappointed, she settled down to regular schoolwork and looked forward to Saturdays, when she could ride the bus downtown to the movies or to the hotel and watch all the action on the street. Servicemen returned to Seattle every day, and many drifted to the labor union office near the hotel.

The newsreel showed the surrender of the Japanese on the USS *Missouri* that was anchored in Tokyo Bay. Laura stayed after the feature movie to watch it again. The Japanese officials wore top hats and tails, as if they were dressed for a fancy ball. They were giving up in style. That fit with the way the Wakamutsus acted and even Miyoko. They had grace and manners that had to have come from their Japanese heritage.

The last Saturday of September, Laura and Eddie made their usual trip downtown. As they walked from the bus stop to the hotel, Laura saw Maude's car pull out from the curb and head their way.

Maude was nowhere in sight. "Somebody's stealing her car!" Laura shouted. She waved her arms at the car, and the man driving pulled over.

"Something wrong?" he called out the window.

The face was oddly familiar, although she didn't know the man.

"Jerry Bowers?" Eddie asked, and Laura knew immediately that he was right.

"Yes. Do I know you?" Jerry asked.

Laura introduced them, and he explained that he'd returned the night before. "Mama's up in the apartment. We stayed up nearly all night talking, so she's slow getting around this morning."

They stepped back so he could move on, and then they rushed up to Maude's apartment to hear all about Jerry's return.

The second week in October, Eddie and Laura were walking home from school when three soldiers got off the bus at the corner ahead of them.

"There are more soldiers around here than you can shake a stick at," Eddie said.

The men had slung huge duffel bags over their shoulders. One man pointed toward their street, and the men turned that direction.

"*Ooh!*" Laura screamed and ran toward the men. "Bruce! Bruce!" The men stopped. One of them turned, and then he dropped his bag and ran toward them. Laura looked back and saw Eddie limping along as fast as he could move.

Of course, she reached her oldest brother first. Bruce hugged her and swung her off her feet. Then he put her down and rushed toward Eddie and gave him the same treatment.

"We didn't know you were coming," Laura said. "Why didn't you call us?"

"I thought I'd surprise the family." He introduced his friends, who had a few hours to spend with the Edwards family before catching the train for their homes, one in Montana, and the other in Idaho.

"Mama will be so surprised," Laura said.

When they got home, no one was there. Laura found a note from Mama on the refrigerator.

"She won't be home until five. She and Margie went downtown." Since war production was over, Margie had been looking for a different job. Laura's dad had been right; Boeing didn't need so many workers. He still worked there, but now he had Sundays off and only worked eight hours a day.

Gary and Ginny came in from school, and the reunion continued. Corrine walked in from the neighbors' and hugged Bruce. She told him all about Neil, who had called several times from a hospital in California.

While they waited, Bruce and the other soldiers lounged in the living room and entertained them with tales about the lighter side of life in the army. Bruce moved over to the couch beside Laura.

"Every morning and every night, I read your bookmark," he told her. "It carried me through the bad parts of the war." He pulled the bookmark from his wallet. It was well worn and creased, but Laura's carefully printed words from the Twenty-third Psalm were still legible.

"God was with me," Bruce said. "I constantly reminded myself of that and of the little girl who wanted to see me in one piece after the war." He tickled her sides. "You have sure grown up in the last few years."

Laura grinned. She was the shortest in her family, but at that moment she felt six feet tall.

"The home front kept us going," one of the soldiers said. "The

Germans were running out of planes and bullets, but our supplies kept on coming."

"We sold war stamps at school," Eddie said.

"All your efforts brought us home," Bruce said. He looked up at the commotion at the door as Mama and Margie carried packages inside. "Hi, Mama," Bruce said as casually as if he'd seen her just that morning.

For an instant, Mama froze. "Oh, Bruce!" she wailed, and it was almost a repetition of the day that Corrine found out that Neil was alive. Mama was still wiping tears of joy when Dad came home.

He shook Bruce's hand and then pulled him close in a bear hug. "Son, we're so glad you're home."

Laura called Yvonne and told her. Yvonne seemed happy, but there was a moment when Laura's happiness was erased. While Yvonne didn't say anything, her tone of voice reminded Laura that Yvonne's brother wouldn't be coming home.

Bruce's friends left that night, and Bruce said he was going to do nothing for a week except sit on the front porch and look at the world from a peaceful view. Eddie tried to get him to talk about D-Day, but Bruce said he couldn't talk about that yet. He wanted to look ahead, not back.

Only a few days had passed before Bruce was applying for temporary work until it was time for the January semester to start at the university, where he could attend on the GI Bill.

"If Uncle Sam wants to pay for my education," Bruce said, "I guess I'll take him up on it."

A few days later, Miyoko received a letter from her father. "He believes he will not be home for some time," she told Laura on the telephone. "But he has received many medals for his bravery. I am honored to be his daughter."

Fall days passed, and October turned to November. With no battle news to report, the newspapers and radio focused on the upcoming war crimes trials in Nuremberg, Germany. Laura was stunned by the charges against the Nazi leaders.

"I'm not going to read the paper ever again," she said after reading about the horrible things they had done. It made her feel that same awful pain in her stomach she'd felt when she saw the concentration camps on the newsreel.

"No need to bury your head in the sand," Bruce said. "We must learn from this so it can never happen again. That's what we fought for."

Dad agreed. "It's fitting that a court settle up the end of the war. That's a civilized way to deal with a disagreement."

Two days before Thanksgiving the Nuremberg Trials began, and the radio newscast was filled with nothing else. But at Laura's house, the trials took a backseat to Neil Palmer's arrival.

Corrine had gone with the Palmers to meet Neil's train, and then they all stopped by the house before taking him home.

He was not like Laura remembered. A very thin man came to the door with his arm possessively around Corrine's shoulders, as if he would never let her go. They sat beside each other on the couch. Corrine smiled and kept her gaze on him even when his parents or someone else spoke.

"He may look a little different, but he's the same man who left here," she said. "I can see it in his eyes."

He lifted Corrine's hand to his lips and kissed it. "You're more beautiful than ever," he said very softly, but Laura, who was sitting on his other side, heard it plainly.

"Tell us about the Bataan Death March," Eddie said.

A cloud passed over Neil's face. "I'd rather we talked about the future than the past right now."

"Okay," Eddie said quickly, and the others respected Neil's wishes, just as they had Bruce's. Talk turned to Thanksgiving, and the Palmers agreed to come to dinner. The Wakamutsu family had been invited to come, as well.

For two days, Laura and the girls cleaned and helped Mama cook. On Thursday morning the family rearranged the Edwardses' living room.

By moving furniture to the edges of the room and putting tables together, Bruce and Gary created one long table. The girls set up the wooden folding chairs they'd borrowed from the church. Mama draped several cloths over the tables, and Laura and Eddie made place mats out of brown construction paper with horns of plenty on the left side. On the right side, they wrote a name, so everyone would know where to sit.

After Mr. and Mrs. Palmer and Neil, Maude and Jerry, and the Wakamutsus and Miyoko arrived, Mama and the girls carried the turkey and all the trimmings to the living room.

"Shall we have grace?" Dad asked. They all took their seats and joined hands. "Father, thank You for another Thanksgiving and this special one when we have so much to be thankful for. We are proud to be Americans and thank You for the freedoms we enjoy. Thank You for keeping our loved ones safe as they faced battle and for bringing them home to us. Amen."

"Amen" echoed around the table.

Laura looked around at her reunited family and added quietly, "God bless America."